The Turner Twins

Ralph Henry Barbour

Alpha Editions

This edition published in 2024

ISBN : 9789362518422

Design and Setting By
Alpha Editions
www.alphaedis.com
Email - info@alphaedis.com

Contents

CHAPTER I
INTRODUCES A PAIR OF HEROES

"Jail," said the boy in the gray flannels.

"School," pronounced the boy in the blue serge.

"Bet you!"

"No, sir, you owe me ten cents now. You didn't pay up the last time."

"It's wrong to bet for money, Ned."

The other set down the suitcase he was carrying and scoffed. "Yes, when you lose," he observed, with deep sarcasm. "That's thirty-five cents you owe me. You bet in Chicago that—"

"That debt's outlawed. Chicago's in Michigan—"

"Bet you!"

"And this is New York, and so—"

"Mighty good thing Dad sent you to school, Laurie. Chicago's in Illinois, you ignoramus."

"Is it? Well, who cares?" Laurence Stenman Turner had also deposited the bag he was carrying on the brick sidewalk and was applying a lavender-bordered handkerchief to a moist brow. "Just the same, that's a jail."

"If that's a jail, I'll eat my hat," declared the other,

"It's not a school, though, and that's flat," was the prompt retort.

"Huh, that was an easy one!" Edward Anderson Turner retreated to a flat-topped stone wall bordering a well-shaded lawn and seated himself with a sigh of relief. His companion followed suit. Behind them, grass and trees and flower beds made a pleasant setting for a square gray house, half hidden from the street. Overhead a horse-chestnut tree spread low branches across the sidewalk. The quiet village street ascended gently, curving as it went, empty in both directions. Somewhere on a neighboring thoroughfare a scissors-grinder was punctuating the silence with the musical *ding—dang—dong* of bells. In a near-by tree a locust was making his shrill clatter. Across the way, the subject of contention, stood a large red-brick edifice, stone trimmed, many windowed, costly and unlovely. The boys viewed it silently. Then their glances fell to the two black suitcases on the curbing.

"How far did that hombre say it was to the school?" asked Ned Turner, after a minute of silence.

"Three quarters of a mile."

"How far have we walked already?"

"Mile and a half."

"Consequently?"

"Said hombre was a li—was unvoracious."

"Un-*ver*-acious is the word, old son."

"What do we care? We don't own it," replied Laurie, cheerfully. "Want to go on?"

Ned shook his head slowly. "What time have you got?" he asked.

"What time do you want?" was the flippant response.

With a sigh, Ned pulled back his left sleeve and looked at his watch. "It's only about a quarter to twelve. We don't have to get there until six if we don't want to."

"I know, but I couldn't sit on this wall all that time! Besides, what about lunch?"

"I'm not very hungry," was the sad reply.

"That's the trouble with having your breakfast late."

"That's the trouble with eating two plates of griddle-cakes, you mean," retorted Laurie. "Anyway, I'm hungry if you're not. Let's go."

But he made no move, and they continued to dangle their shoes from the wall and gaze lazily across the shady street. The scissors-grinder's chime died in the distance. Farther down the street the whirring of a lawn-mower competed with the locust.

"Upon a wall they sat them down," murmured Ned, turning a challenging look on his companion.

"Lost in the wilds of Orstead Town," added Laurie.

Ned nodded mild approval and once more silence held.

Save that one was dressed in gray and the other in blue, the two boys were strikingly alike. Each was slim of body and round of face, with red-brown hair and a short, slightly impertinent nose. Ned's eyes were a trifle bluer than Laurie's and he had the advantage—if advantage it was—of some five pounds of weight. But neither of these facts was apparent at first glance. Faces and hands were well browned and the pair looked extremely healthy. They were dressed neatly, with perhaps more attention to detail than is usual in lads of their age, their attire terminating at one end in well-polished brown shoes and at the other in immaculate black derbies. Their age was fifteen years, three months, and eleven days. Which, of course, leads you to the correct conclusion that they were twins.

"Maybe," hazarded Laurie, presently, "we've lost our way."

"Don't just see how we could," Ned objected. "The old chap at the station said we were to keep right along up Walnut Street. This is still Walnut Street, isn't it?"

"I suppose so." Laurie's glance strayed right and left. "Must be; I don't see any walnuts."

"Guess the only 'nuts' are right here. Come on, let 's hit the trail again." Ned slid to his feet and took up his burden. "Why the dickens we didn't take that carriage the fellow wanted to sell us is more than I see."

"'Cause we needed the exercise. Also, 'cause we're down to a dollar and fourteen cents between us—unless you 're holding out."

"Well, I'm not!" replied Ned, indignantly. "I paid for the breakfasts in New York—"

"And I paid for dinner on the diner last night—"

"Who said you didn't?" They went on leisurely, and presently Ned continued: "Say, suppose we don't like this ranch after we get there—then what, old son?"

Laurie considered thoughtfully. Then, "Two things we can do," he pronounced. "No, three. We can put up with it, change it to suit us, or leave it."

"Leave it! Yes, we can! On a dollar and fourteen cents?"

"We'll have nearly twenty more when we cash Dad's check and pay the term bill. Twenty dollars would take us back to New York and buy a lot of griddle-cakes, anyway."

Laurie's voice was partly drowned by a small delivery automobile that dashed into sight at a corner ahead and sped by with a clamor worthy of a four-ton truck. The brothers looked after it interestedly. "That's the first sign of life we've seen," said Ned. "Say, I do wish this street would stop twisting this way. First thing we know, we'll be back at the station!"

"Bet you I'd hop the first freight then. I've got a hunch that we're not going to care for Hillman's School."

"Speak for yourself. I am. I like this town, too. It's pretty."

"Oh, it's pretty enough," grumbled Laurie, "but it went to sleep about a century ago and hasn't waked up since. Here's somebody coming; let's ask where the school is."

"It's just a girl."

"What of it? She probably knows."

The girl appeared to be of about their own age and wore a white middy dress with black trimming and a scarlet tie knotted below a V of sun-browned throat. She wore no hat and her dark hair was gathered into a single braid. As she drew near she gave the boys a quick glance of appraisal from a pair of gravely friendly brown eyes. It was Ned who shifted his suitcase to his left hand and raised his derby. It was always Ned who spoke first; after that, they alternated scrupulously.

"Would you please tell us where Hillman's School is?" he asked.

The girl stopped and her somewhat serious face lighted with a smile. "It's right there," she replied, and nodded.

The boys turned to the blankness of a high privet hedge behind an iron fence. The girl laughed softly. "Behind the hedge, I mean," she explained. "The gate is a little way around the corner there, on Summit Street."

"Oh," said Laurie. That laugh was contagious, and he grinned in response. "A man at the station told us it was only three quarters of a mile, but we've been walking for hours!"

"I guess it's nearer a mile than three quarters," answered the girl, slowly. She appeared to be giving the matter very serious consideration and two little thoughtful creases appeared above her nose, a small, straight nose that was bridged by a sprinkling of freckles. Then the smile came again. "Maybe it did seem longer, though," she acknowledged, "for it's uphill all the way; and then, you had your bags. You're new boys, aren't you?"

Ned acknowledged it, adding, "Think we'll like it?"

The girl seemed genuinely surprised. "Why, of course! Every one likes it. What a perfectly funny idea!"

"Well," said Laurie, defensively, "we've never tried boarding-school before, you see. Dad didn't know anything about Hillman's, either. He chose it on account of the way the advertisement read in a magazine. Something about 'a moderate discipline rigidly enforced.'"

The girl laughed again. (She had a jolly sort of laugh, they decided.) "You're—you're twins, aren't you?" she asked.

"He is," replied Ned, gravely.

"Why—why, aren't you both?" Her brown eyes grew very round and the little lines creased her nose again.

"It's this way," explained Laurie. "Ned was born first, and so, as there was only one of him, he wasn't a twin. Then I came, and that made two of us, and I was a twin. You see, don't you? It's really quite plain."

The girl shook her head slowly in puzzlement. "I—I'm afraid I don't," she answered apologetically. "You *must* be twins—both of you, I mean—because you both look just like both—I mean, each other!" Then she caught the sparkle of mischief in Ned's blue eyes and laughed. Then they all laughed. After which they seemed suddenly to be very good friends, such good friends that Laurie abandoned custom and spoke out of turn.

"I suppose you know a lot of the fellows," he said.

The girl shook her head. "N—no, not any, really. Of course, I see most of them when they come to Mother's, but she doesn't like me to—to *know* them."

"Of course not," approved Ned. "She's dead right, too. They're a pretty poor lot, I guess."

"Oh, no, they're not, really! Only, you see—" She stopped, and then went on a trifle breathlessly: "I guess she wouldn't be awfully pleased if she saw me now! I—I hope you'll like the school."

She nodded and went on.

"Thanks," called Laurie. "If we don't like it, we'll change it. Good-by."

"Nice kid," observed Ned, tolerantly, as they turned the corner of the hedge. "Wonder who she is. She said most of the fellows went to her mother's. Maybe her mother gives dancing lessons or something, eh?"

"If she does, she won't see me," responded his brother, firmly. "No dancing for mine."

"Maybe it's compulsory."

"Maybe it's esthetic," retorted Laurie, derisively. "It makes no never mind. I'm agin it. This must be the place. Yes, there's a sign."

It was a very modest sign a-swing from a rustic post beside a broad entrance giving on to a well-kept drive. "Hillman's School—Entrance Only," it read. Laurie stopped in pretended alarm and laid a detaining clutch on Ned's shoulder.

"'Entrance Only'! Sounds as if we couldn't ever get out again, Ned! Do you dare?"

Ned looked doubtfully through at the curving drive and the red-brick building that showed beyond the border of trees and shrubbery. Then he threw back his shoulders and set foot bravely within.

"Come, comrade, let us know the worst!"

Laurie, with a gesture of resignation, followed.

"What you durst I will likewise durst!"

CHAPTER II
THE GIRL IN THE WHITE MIDDY

When Doctor John Hyde Hillman started a modest school for boys, on the bank of the Hudson River, at Orstead, the town barely crept to the one brick building that contained dormitory and recitation-rooms. But that was nearly twenty years ago, and to-day the place is no longer isolated, but stands well inside the residence section of the village. There are four buildings, occupying most of an unusually large block. School Hall, four stories in height, is a red-brick, slate-roofed edifice, whose unloveliness has been mercifully hidden by ivy. It faces Summit Street and contains the class-rooms, the offices, and, at one end, the principal's quarters. Flanking it are the two dormitories, East Hall and West Hall. These, while of brick too, are modern and far more attractive. Each contains sleeping-rooms to accommodate forty students, two masters' studies, a recreation-hall, dining-room, kitchen, and service-rooms. Behind East Hall is the gymnasium, a picturesque structure of random-set stone, gray stucco, and much glass. Here, besides the gymnasium proper, is an auditorium of good size, a modest swimming-tank, locker-room and baths, and a commodious office presided over by Mr. Wells, the physical director. From the gymnasium steps one looks across an attractive, well-kept quadrangle of shaded turf, vegetable and flower gardens, and tennis-courts.

Doctor Hillman occupies an apartment at the west end of the School Hall, gained from the building by way of the school offices, and from without by way of a wide porch, vine screened in summer and glassed in winter, an outdoor living-room where, on seasonable Friday afternoons, the doctor's maiden sister, Miss Tabitha, who keeps house for him, serves weak tea and layer-cake to all comers. Miss Tabitha, I regret to say, is known among the boys as "Tabby," with, however, no more intention of disrespect than in alluding to the doctor as "Johnny." Miss Tabitha's thin body holds a warm heart, and her somewhat stern countenance belies her kindly ways.

On this fifteenth day of September, shortly after twelve o'clock, Miss Tabitha was seated on the vine-shaded porch in an erect and uncompromising attitude, her knitting-needles clicking busily. Near by, but a few moments before released from the office, the doctor was stretched in a long wicker chair, a morning paper before him. At the other end of the porch, a gate-legged table was spread for the mid-day meal, and a middle-aged colored woman—who, when it pleased her, answered to the name of Aunt Persis—shuffled in and out of sight at intervals. It was Miss Tabitha who, hearing the sound of steps on the walk, peered over her glasses and broke the silence.

"Two more of the boys are coming, John," she announced.

The doctor grunted.

"I think they are new boys. Yes, I am sure they are. And bless my soul, John, they're alike as two peas!"

"Alike?" The doctor rustled the paper to indicate interest. "Well, why shouldn't they be? Probably they're brothers. Let me see, weren't those two boys from California brothers? Of course. Turner's the name."

"Well, I never saw two boys so much alike in all my born days," Miss Tabitha marveled. "Do you suppose they can be twins, John?"

"It's quite within the realm of probability," was the reply. "I believe that twins do occur occasionally, even in the—er—best-regulated families."

"Well, they certainly *are* twins!" Miss Tabitha laid down her work, brushed the front of her immaculate dress, and prepared to rise. "I suppose I had better go and meet them," she added.

"I don't see the necessity for it, my dear," the doctor protested. "Cummins may, I think, be relied on to deal even with—er—twins."

"Of course; but—still—California's such a long way—and they may feel strange—or lonesome—"

The doctor laughed gently. "Then by all means go, my dear. If you like, have them out here for a few minutes. If the resemblance between them is as striking as you seem to think, they must be worth seeing."

When Miss Tabitha had tripped into the house, the doctor dropped his paper, stretched luxuriously, and, with a sigh of protest, sat up. He was several years younger than his sister—which is to say, in the neighborhood of forty-seven. He was a smallish man, compactly built, with a pleasant countenance on which a carefully-trimmed Vandyke beard made up to an extent for the lack of hair above. He wore shell-rimmed glasses and was very near-sighted, a fact emphasized by his manner of thrusting his head forward to eke out the deficiencies of his lenses. This trick was apparent a minute later when, following in the tripping footsteps of Miss Tabitha, the two boys emerged on the porch. They were amazingly alike, the doctor decided: same height, same breadth at hip and shoulder, same coloring, same leisurely, yet confident, ease of movement, same expression of lively curiosity twinkling through an almost depressingly respectful solemnity.

"These are the Turner boys," announced Miss Tabitha. "This is Edward and this is—" She halted to look doubtfully from one to the other. "Or—or perhaps *this* is Edward and—Dear me!"

"I'm Edward, ma'am," said the boy in blue.

"Well, I don't see how you can ever be *certain* of it!" sighed Miss Tabitha, doubtfully. "This is Doctor Hillman."

They shook hands, and in a moment the boys found themselves seated side by side and replying to the doctor's questions.

"You are entering with certificates from your high school principal, I believe, young gentlemen. What year were you?"

"Second, sir," answered Ned.

"And your home is in—"

"Santa Lucia, sir," replied Laurie.

"California," added Ned.

"Well, you're quite a ways from home. Did you make the trip alone?"

"Yes, sir. Dad was coming with us as far as Chicago, but something happened so he couldn't. We didn't have any trouble, though."

"Really? Well, I believe you have the distinction of residing farther away than any of your fellows here. I don't recall any one who lives as far away as California; do you, sister?"

Miss Tabitha looked doubtful and hesitated an instant before she replied, "George Watson comes from Wyoming, I think, John."

"So he does," assented the doctor, gravely; "but measured in a straight line, my dear, California is slightly farther than Wyoming."

"Is it?" asked Miss Tabitha, untroubled. "I never could remember where those western States are."

"You remember many more important things, however. My sister, boys, fancied that she detected a certain resemblance between you, and even surmised that you might be—er—twins. Doubtless she's mistaken."

"No, sir," answered Ned, more than a trace of surprise in his voice. "I mean, we are twins, sir."

"Why, now that's interesting! Looking closer—" the doctor leaned forward and craned his head—"I believe I detect a certain slight similarity myself!"

There was a perceptible twinkle behind the glasses and Laurie dared a laugh, in which the doctor and Ned joined, while Miss Tabitha murmured: "Well! I should think you *might!*"

"I hope you are both going to like the school," continued the doctor. "Of course, you'll find our ways a little different, but we'll try to make you feel at home. You are the first representatives of your State who have attended our school, and I trust that both in conduct and industry you will bring honor to it. Mr. Cornish, your hall master, will advise you in all matters pertaining to your studies, Other questions may be taken to Mr. Cummins, the school secretary, whom you have doubtless already met. But I want you always to feel at perfect liberty to come to me at any time on any matter at all. And," added the doctor, with a twinkle, "if we fail you, there is still my sister, who, I assure you, possesses more wisdom than all of us."

Miss Tabitha acknowledged the compliment with a little wry smile, and Ned and Laurie arose.

"Yes, sir," said the former.

"Thank you, sir," said Laurie.

"Luncheon is served at one in West Hall," continued the doctor. "That's the dormitory behind you there. Beginning with supper to-night, you will take your meals in your own hall, but only a few of the students have arrived as yet, and so only one dining-room is open. I'm very glad to have met you, young gentlemen. Mr. Cummins will direct you to your room. Good morning."

Five minutes later, the Turner twins set their suitcases down on the floor of Number 16 East Hall and looked about them. Number 16 was not palatial as to size, but it was big enough to hold comfortably the two single beds, the study-table, the two narrow chiffoniers, and the four chairs that made up its furnishing. There was a generous-sized closet at each side of the door, and two windows set close together between the beds. Under the windows was a wide seat, lacking only pillows to make it inviting. From the casements the boys looked over or through the topmost branches of the maples that lined Washington Street and followed Summit Street as it continued its ascent of the hill and presently leveled out between a thick wood on one side and an open field on the other.

"That must be the athletic field," said Laurie. "See the stand there? And the goal-posts? How do you like it?"

"The field? Looks all right from here."

"I mean the whole outfit, you simp; the school and Doctor Hillman and Miss Frosty-Face and everything."

"Cut out calling names, Laurie. Miss Hillman's all right. So's the doctor. So's the school. I like it. Wonder when our trunks will get here."

"Half an hour ago you had a hunch you weren't going to like it," jeered Laurie. "Changed your mind, haven't you?"

"Yes, and I'm going to change more than my mind." Whereupon Ned opened his bag and selected a clean shirt. "What time is it?"

"What do you wear a watch for if you never look at it?" grumbled his brother. "It's ten to one, Lazy. I'm going to find a place to wash up. I choose this side of the room, Ned."

Ned studied the room a moment. "No, you don't," he challenged. "I'll take this side. I'm the oldest." "There isn't any difference, you chump. One side's as good as the other."

"Then you won't mind taking the other," answered Ned, sweetly. "Run along and find the lavatory. I think it's at the head of the stairs. Wonder why they put us up two flights."

"Guess they knew you were naturally lazy and needed the exercise."

Laurie dodged a pair of traveling slippers in a red-leather case and disappeared into the corridor.

Some ten minutes later they descended the stairway together and set out for West Hall. Laurie drew attention to the gymnasium building, but Ned, who had recovered his appetite, only deigned it a glance. Two boys, luggage laden, evidently just arrived, came down the steps of School Hall as the twins passed, and stared curiously.

"Guess they've never seen twins before in this part of the world," grumbled Laurie. "Those chaps nearly popped their eyes out!"

West Hall proved an exact duplicate of their own dormitory, and the dining-room occupied all the right end of it. There were about fifteen boys there, in age varying from fourteen to eighteen, and there was a perceptible pause in the business of eating when the newcomers entered. A waitress conducted them to seats at a table already occupied by three other lads, and asked if they'd have milk or iced tea. Ned, as usual, answered for both.

"Iced tea, please, and lots of lemon."

A very stout boy, sitting across the table, sniggered, and then, encountering Ned's inquiring regard, said, "Guess you think you're in the Waldorf!"

"What's the Waldorf?" asked Ned. "Don't you get lemon with iced tea here?"

"Sure! but you don't get much. Say, are you fellows—twins, or what?"

"Twins?" repeated Laurie. "Where do you get that stuff? This fellow's name is Anderson and mine's Stenman. What's yours?"

"Crow. Honest, is that a fact?" Crow looked appealingly at the other occupants of the table. These, however, two rather embarrassed-looking youngsters of fourteen or thereabouts, fixed their eyes on their plates, and Crow turned his regard incredulously back to the twins. "Gee, you fellows look enough alike to be—be—" He swallowed the word. "Aren't you even related?"

Ned gazed speculatively at Laurie and Laurie gazed speculatively at Ned. "We might be," hazarded the latter.

Laurie nodded. "If we went back far enough, we might find a common ancestor."

The arrival of luncheon caused a diversion, although Crow, who was a round-faced, credulous-looking youth of perhaps seventeen, continued to regard them surreptitiously and in puzzlement. At last, making the passing of the salt an excuse, for further conversation, he asked, "Where do you fellows come from?"

"California," said Ned.

"Santa Lucia," said Laurie.

"Well, but," sputtered Crow, "isn't California in Santa—I mean, isn't Santa— Say, you guys are joking, I'll bet!"

"Methinks," observed Ned, helping himself gravely to mustard, "his words sound coarse and vulgar."

Laurie abstractedly added a fourth teaspoon of sugar to his iced tea. "Like Turk or Kurd or even Bulgar," he murmured.

Crow stared, grunted, and pushed his chair back. "You fellows think you're smart, don't you?" he sputtered. "Bet you you are twins—both of you!"

Ned and Laurie looked after him in mild and patient surprise until his broad back had disappeared from view. Then a choking sound came from one of the younger lads, and Ned asked gently, "Now what's your trouble, son?"

The boy grew very red of face and gave way to giggles. "I knew all the time you were twins," he gasped.

"Did you really?" exclaimed Laurie. "Well, listen. Just as a favor to us, don't say anything about it, eh? You see, we're sort of—sort of—"

"Sort of sensitive," aided Ned. "We'd rather it wasn't generally known. You understand, don't you?"

The boy looked as if he was very far indeed from understanding, but he nodded, choked again, and muttered something that seemed to indicate that the secret was safe with him. Laurie thanked him gratefully.

After luncheon they went sight-seeing about the school, snooped through the dim corridors and empty class-rooms of School Hall, viewed the gymnasium and experimented with numerous apparatus, and finally, after browsing through a flower and vegetable garden behind the recitation building and watching two boys make a pretense of playing tennis, returned to Number 16 in the hope of finding their trunks. But the baggage had not arrived, and presently, since the room was none too cool, they descended again and followed the curving drive to the right and past a sign that said "Exit Only" and wandered west on Summit Street.

For the middle of September in the latitude of southern New York the weather was decidedly warm, and neither grass nor trees hinted that autumn had arrived. In the well-kept gardens across the way, scarlet sage and cosmos, asters and dahlias made riots of color.

"Hot!" grunted Ned, running a finger around the inside of his collar.

"Beastly," agreed Laurie, removing his cap and fanning his heated face. "Wonder where the river is. If we had our bathing-suits, maybe we could go for a swim."

"Yes, and if we had a cake of ice we could sit on it!" responded Ned, sarcastically. "This place is hotter than Santa Lucia."

At the next corner they turned again to the right. Morton Street, like so many of the streets in Orstead, refused to go straight, and after a few minutes, to their mild bewilderment, they found themselves on Walnut Street once more, a block below the school.

"I'm not going back yet," said Laurie, firmly. "Let's find a place where we can get something cool to drink."

As Walnut Street was unpromising, they crossed it and meandered along Garden Street. The houses here appeared to be less prosperous, and the front yards were less likely to hold lawn and flowers than dilapidated baby-carriages. At the first crossing they peered right and left, and were rewarded by the sight of a swinging sign at a little distance.

What the sign said was as yet a mystery, for the trees intervened, but Laurie declared that he believed in signs and they made their way toward it. It finally proved to be a very cheerful little sign hung above a little white door in a little pale-blue two-story house, the lower floor of which was plainly devoted to commercial purposes.

L. S. DEANE

BOOKS, TOYS, AND

CONFECTIONERY

CIRCULATING LIBRARY

LAUNDRY AGENCY

TONICS

That is what the sign said in red letters on a white background. The windows, many paned, allowed uncertain glimpses of various articles: tops of red and blue and green, boxes of pencils, pads of paper, jars of candy, many bottles of ink, a catcher's glove, a dozen tennis-balls, some paper kites—

Laurie dragged Ned inside, through a screen door that, on opening, caused a bell to tinkle somewhere in the farther recesses of the little building. It was dark inside, after the glare of the street, and refreshingly cool. Laurie, leading the way, collided with a bench, caromed off the end of a counter, and became aware of a figure, dimly seen, beyond the width of a show-case.

"Have you anything cold to drink?" asked Ned, leaning across the show-case.

"Ginger-ale or tonic or something?" Laurie elaborated.

"Yes, indeed," replied the apparition, in a strangely familiar voice. "If you will step over to the other side, please—"

Ned and Laurie leaned farther across the show-case.

It was the girl in the white middy dress.

CHAPTER III
CAKES AND ALE

"Hello!" exclaimed the twins, in one voice.

"Hello," replied the girl, and they suspected that she was smiling, although their eyes were still too unused to the dimness of the little store for them to be certain. She was still only a vague figure in white, with a deeper blur where her face should have been. Treading on each other's heels, Ned and Laurie followed her to the other side. The twilight brightened and objects became more distinct. They were in front of a sort of trough-like box in which, half afloat in a pool of ice-water, were bottles of tonic and soda and ginger-ale. Behind it was a counter on which reposed a modest array of pastry.

"What do you want?" asked the girl in the middy.

"Ginger-ale," answered Ned. "Say, do you live here?"

"No, this is the shop," was the reply. "I live upstairs."

"Oh, well, you know what I mean," muttered Ned. "Is this your store?"

"It's my mother's. I help in it afternoons. My mother is Mrs. Deane. The boys call her the Widow. I'm Polly Deane."

"Pleased to know you," said Laurie. "Our name's Turner. I'm Laurie and he's Ned. Let me open that for you."

"Oh, no, thanks. I've opened hundreds of them. Oh dear! You said ginger-ale, didn't you! And I've opened a root-beer. It's so dark in here in the afternoon."

"That's all right," Ned assured her. "We like root-beer. We'd just as soon have it as ginger-ale. Wouldn't we, Laurie?"

"You bet! We're crazy about it."

"Are you sure? It's no trouble to—Well, *this* is ginger-ale, anyway. I'm awfully sorry!"

"What do we care?" asked Ned. "We don't own it."

"Don't own it?" repeated Polly, in a puzzled tone.

"That's just an expression of his," explained Laurie. "He's awfully slangy. I try to break him of it, but it's no use. It's fierce."

"Of course *you* don't use slang?" asked Polly, demurely. "Who wants the root-beer?"

"You take it," said Laurie, hurriedly.

"No, you," said Ned. "You're fonder of it than I am, Laurie. I don't mind, really!"

Laurie managed a surreptitious kick on his brother's shin. "Tell you what," he exclaimed, "we'll mix 'em!"

Ned agreed, though not enthusiastically, and with the aid of a third glass the deed was done. The boys tasted experimentally, each asking a question over the rim of his glass. Then looks of relief came over both faces and they sighed ecstatically.

"Corking!" they breathed in unison.

Polly laughed, "I never knew any one to do that before," she said. "I'm glad you like it. I'll tell the other boys about it."

"No, you mustn't," protested Ned. "It's our invention. We'll call it—call it—"

"Call it an Accident," suggested Laurie.

"We'll call it a Polly," continued the other. "It really is bully. It's—it's different; isn't it, Laurie? Have another?"

"Who were those on?" was the suspicious reply.

"You. The next is on me. Only maybe another wouldn't taste so good, eh?"

"Don't you fool yourself! I'll risk that."

However, the third and fourth bottles, properly combined though they were, lacked novelty, and it was some time before the last glass was emptied. Meanwhile, of course, they talked. The boys acknowledged that, so far, they liked what they had seen of the school. Mention of the doctor and Miss Hillman brought forth warm praise from Polly. "Every one likes the doctor ever so much," she declared. "And Miss Tabitha is—"

"Miss what?" interrupted Laurie.

"Miss Tabitha. That's her name." Polly laughed softly. "They call her Tabby,—the boys, I mean,—but they like her. She's a dear, even if she does look sort of—of cranky. She isn't, though, a bit. She makes believe she's awfully stern, but she's just as soft as—as—"

"As Laurie's head?" offered Ned, helpfully. "Say, you sell 'most everything here, don't you? Are those cream-puffs?"

Ned slipped a hand into his pocket and Laurie coughed furiously. Ned's hand came forth empty. He turned away from temptation. "They look mighty good," he said. "If we'd seen those before we'd had all that ginger-ale—"

Polly spoke detachedly. "You can have credit if you like," she said, placing the empty bottles aside. "The doctor lets the boys run bills here up to a dollar. They can't go over a dollar, though."

"Personally," observed Laurie, jingling some coins in a trousers pocket, "I prefer to pay cash. Still, there are times—"

"Yes, a fellow gets short now and then," said Ned, turning for another look at the pastry counter. "Maybe, just for—for convenience, it would be a good plan to have an account here, Laurie. Sometimes a fellow forgets to put any money in his pocket, you know. Does your mother make these?"

"Yes, the cream-cakes, and some of the others. The rest Miss Comfort makes."

"That's another funny name," said Laurie. "Who is Miss Comfort?"

"She's—she's just Miss Comfort, I guess," replied Polly. "She lives on the next corner, in the house with the white shutters. She's quite old, almost seventy, I suppose, and she makes the nicest cake in Orstead. Everybody goes to her for cakes. That's the way she lives, I guess."

"Maybe we'd ought to help her," suggested Ned, mentally choosing the largest and fattest cakes on the tray. "I guess we'll take a couple. How much are they?"

"Six cents apiece," said Polly. "Do you want them in a bag?"

"No, thanks." Ned handed one of the cakes to Laurie; "we'll eat them now." Then, between mouthfuls; "Maybe you'd better charge this to us. If we're going to open an account, we might as well do it now, don't you think?"

Polly retired behind a counter and produced a long and narrow book, from which dangled a lead pencil at the end of a string. She put the tip of the pencil between her lips and looked across. "You'd better tell me your full names, I think."

"Edward Anderson Turner and—"

"I meant just your first names."

"Oh! Edward and Laurence. You can charge us each with two bottles and one cake."

"I like that!" scoffed Laurie. "Thought you were treating to cakes?"

"Huh! Don't you want to help Miss Comfort? I should think you'd like to— to do a charitable act once in a while."

"Don't see what difference it makes to her," grumbled Laurie, "whether you pay for both or I pay for one. She gets her money just the same."

Ned brushed a crumb from his jacket. "You don't get the idea," he replied gently. "Of course, I might pay for both, but you wouldn't feel right about it, Laurie."

"Wouldn't I? Where do you get that stuff? You try it and see." Laurie spoke grimly, but not hopefully. Across the counter, Polly was giggling over the account-book.

"You're the funniest boys I ever did see," she explained, in answer to their inquiring looks. "You—you say such funny things!"

Before she could elucidate, footsteps sounded in the room behind the store and a tiny white-haired woman appeared. In spite of her hair, she couldn't have been very old, for her face was plump and unwrinkled and her cheeks quite rosy. Seeing the customers, she bowed prettily and said "Good afternoon" in a very sweet voice.

"Good afternoon," returned the twins.

"Mama, these are the Turner boys," said Polly. "One of them is Ned and the other is Laurie, but I don't know which, because they look just exactly alike. They—they're twins!"

"I want to know!" said Mrs. Deane. "Isn't that nice? I'm very pleased to meet you, young gentlemen. I hope Polly has served you with what you wanted. My stock is kind of low just now. You see, we don't have many customers in summer, and it's very hard to get things, nowadays, even if you do pay three times what they're worth. Polly, those ice-cream cones never did come, did they?"

"Gee, do you have ice-cream?" asked Ned; eagerly.

"Never you mind!" said Laurie, grabbing his arm. "You come on out of here before you die on my hands. I'm sorry to tell you, ma'am, that he doesn't know when to stop eating. I have to go around everywhere with him and look after him. If I didn't, he'd be dead in no time."

"I want to know!" exclaimed the Widow Deane interestedly. "Why, it's very fortunate for him he has you, isn't it?"

"Yes'm," answered Laurie, but he spoke doubtfully, for the little white-haired lady seemed to hide a laugh behind her words. Ned was grinning. Laurie propelled him to the door. Then, without relinquishing his grasp, he doffed his cap.

"Good afternoon," he said, "We'll come again,"

"We know not how," added Ned, "we know not when."

"Bless my soul!" murmured the Widow, as the screen door swung behind them.

Back at school, the twins found a different scene from what they had left. The grounds were populous with boys, and open windows in the two dormitory buildings showed many others. The entrances were piled with trunks and more were arriving. A rattling taxi turned in at the gate, with much blowing of a frenzied but bronchial horn, and added five merry youths to the population. Ned and Laurie made their way to East Hall, conscious, as they approached, of many eyes focussed on them from wide-flung windows. Remarks reached them, too.

"See who's with us!" came from a second-floor casement above the entrance; "the two Dromios!"

"Tweedledum and Tweedledee!"

"The Siamese Twins, I'll bet a cooky!"

"Hi, East Hall! Heads out!"

The two were glad when they reached the shelter of the doorway. "Some one's going to get his head punched before long," growled Ned, as they started upstairs.

"What do we care? We don't own 'em. Let them have their fun, Neddie."

"I'll let some of them have a wallop," was the answer. "You'd think we were the first pair of twins they'd ever seen!"

"Well, maybe we are. How do you know? Suppose those trunks have come?"

They had, and for the next hour the twins were busy unpacking and getting settled. From beyond their door came sounds of much turmoil; the noise of arriving baggage, the banging of doors, shouts, whistling, singing; but they were otherwise undisturbed until, just when Laurie had slammed down the lid of his empty trunk, there came a knock at their portal, followed, before either one could open his mouth in response, by the appearance in the doorway of a bulky apparition in a gorgeous crimson bath-robe.

"Hello, fellows!" greeted the apparition. "Salutations and everything!"

"Hello, fellows! Salutations and everything!"

CHAPTER IV
KEWPIE STARTS SOMETHING

The twins stared silently and suspiciously for an instant. Then Ned made cautious response.

"Hello," he said, with what must have seemed to the visitor a lamentable lack of cordiality.

The latter pushed the door shut behind him by the kick of one stockinged foot, and grinned jovially. "My name's Proudtree," he announced.

"You can't blame us," replied Laurie, coldly.

Proudtree laughed amiably. "It is a rotten name, isn't it? I live across the corridor, you know. Thought I'd drop in and get acquainted, seeing you're new fellows; extend the hand of friendship and all that. You understand. By Jove, Pringle was right, too!"

"That's fine," said Ned, with more than a trace of sarcasm. "What about?"

"Why," answered Proudtree, easing his generous bulk into a chair, "he said you fellows were twins."

"Not only were," said Laurie, gently, "but are. Don't mind, do you?"

"Oh, come off your horse," begged the visitor. "Don't be so cocky. Who's said anything? I just wanted to have a look. Never saw any twins before—grown-up twins, I mean. You understand."

"Thought you said you came to extend the hand of friendship," retorted Ned, sarcastically. "Well, have a good look, partner. There's no charge!"

Proudtree grinned and accepted the invitation. Ned fumed silently under the inspection, but Laurie's sense of humor came to his aid. Proudtree appeared to be getting a lot of entertainment from his silent comparison of his hosts, and presently, when Ned's exasperation had just about reached the explosive point, he chuckled.

"I've got it," he said.

"Got what?" Laurie asked.

"The—the clue! I know how to tell you apart! His eyes are different from yours; more blue. Yours are sort of gray. But, geewhillikins, it must be a heap of fun! Being twins, I mean. And fooling people. You understand."

"Well, if you're quite through," snapped Ned, "maybe you'll call it a day. We've got things to do."

"Meaning you'd like me to beat it?" asked the visitor, good-temperedly.

"Just that!"

"Oh, come, Ned," Laurie protested, soothingly, "he's all right. I dare say we are sort of freakish and—"

"Sure," agreed Proudtree, eagerly, "that's what I meant. But say, I didn't mean to hurt any one's feelings. Geewhillikins, if I got waxy every time the fellows josh me about being fat—" Words failed him and he sighed deeply.

Laurie laughed. "We might start a side-show, the three of us, and make a bit of money. 'Only ten cents! One dime! This way to the Siamese Twins and the Fat Boy! Walk up! Walk up!'"

Proudtree smiled wanly. "I only weigh a hundred and seventy-eight and three quarters, too," he said dolorously. "If I was a couple of inches taller it wouldn't be so bad."

"I don't think it's bad as it is," said Laurie, kindly. "You don't look really *fat*; you just look sort of—of—"

"Amplitudinous," supplied Ned, with evident satisfaction.

Proudtree viewed him doubtfully. Then he smiled. "Well, I've got to get rid of nearly fifteen pounds in the next two weeks," he said, with a shake of his head, "and that's going to take some doing."

"What for?" Laurie asked. "Why destroy your symmetry?"

"Football. I'm trying for center. I nearly made it last year, but Wiggins beat me out. He's gone now, though, and Mulford as good as said last spring that I could make it this fall if I could get down to a hundred and sixty-five."

"Who's Mulford?" inquired Ned. "A fortune-teller?"

Proudtree ignored the sarcasm. "Mulford's our coach. He's all right, too. The trouble with me is, I'm awfully fond of sweet things, and I—I've been eating a lot of 'em lately. But I guess I can drop fourteen pounds if I cut out pies and candy and things. Don't you think so?" Proudtree appealed to Laurie almost pathetically.

"Don't let any one tell you anything different," replied Laurie, reassuringly. Ned, evidently recovered from his peevishness, asked:

"What sort of football do they play here?"

"Corking!" answered Proudtree.

"I mean, Rugby or the other?"

"Rugby!" exclaimed Proudtree, scornfully. "I guess not! We play regular football. Nobody plays Rugby around these parts. Are you fellows going out?"

"Not just yet," replied Ned.

"He means are we going to try for the football team," explained Laurie. "Yes, we are, Proudtree; at least, one of us is."

"You?"

"We haven't decided yet. You see, we've never played your kind of football. Back home, at high school, we played American Rugby, and it's quite different. But we decided that one of us had better go in for football and the other for baseball, if only to do our duty by the school."

Proudtree looked puzzled. "How are you going to decide?" he asked.

"Oh, we'll toss up or draw lots or something, I suppose. Maybe, though, Ned had better play football, because I know more baseball than he does. Still, I'm not particular."

"That's the limit!" chuckled the visitor. "Say, what are your names? I didn't see any cards on the door."

"Turner. His is Laurie and mine's Ned," answered the latter. "Do we put our names on the door?"

"It's the best way," answered Proudtree. "Well, I've got to be moving. I started to take a shower and got side-tracked. You chaps come on over and see me and I'll get some of the other fellows in. You want to meet the right sort, you know. What's your class?"

"Lower middle, I reckon," said Ned. "That's what we expect."

"Too bad you can't make upper. That's mine. We've got a corking bunch of fellows this year. Well, see you later. Try for Mr. Barrett's table when you go down. That's the best. Maybe they'll put you there if you bluff it out. You understand. So long, fellows."

Proudtree withdrew with considerable dignity in view of his bulk, waving a benedictory hand ere the door closed behind him. Ned shook his head. "Sort of a fresh hombre," he said.

"Oh, he only meant to be friendly, I reckon," said Laurie. "You understand."

Ned laughed. "I'll bet they've got a wonderful football team here if he plays on it! By the way, maybe we'd better settle which of us is to be the football star. I suppose they begin to practise pretty soon. I'll be the goat, if you like; though you had better luck with that book you bought in Chicago. I couldn't make head or tail of it. I never saw so many rules for playing one game in my life!"

"It *was* sort of difficult," agreed Laurie. "I dare say, though, that you pick up the rules quick enough when you start to play. If you don't really mind, I think you'd better go in for football, and I'll do the baseball stunt. I've played it more than you have, you know, even if I'm no wonder."

"All right!" Ned sighed. "We'll get a bottle of arnica to-morrow. Nothing like being prepared. How about going to see Mr. What's-his-name before supper about courses?"

"Might as well, and have it over with. I'd like to know whether we're going to make the lower middle."

"Don't see what else we can make. They can't stick us in the junior class. Where's my coat? For the love of lemons, Laurie, can't you find anything else to sit on? Gosh, look at the wrinkles!"

"Those aren't wrinkles; they're just creases. Come on!"

Half an hour later they closed the door of Mr. Cornish's study on the floor below, in a chastened mood. Each carried a little buff card whereon the instructor had tabulated an amazing number and variety of study periods. Back in Number 16, Ned cast himself into a chair, thrust his legs forth, and gazed disconsolately at the card.

"I don't see where a fellow finds time for anything but work here," he complained. "Sixteen, eighteen, twenty-one hours a week! What do you know about that?"

"Well, don't be so proud of it. I've got the same, haven't I? I wonder how many hours he thinks there are in a day?"

"I tell you what I think," said Ned, after a moment's thought. "I think he got it into his head that we're very ambitious and want to graduate next spring!"

"Maybe that's it," agreed Laurie, gravely. "Shall we go back and tell him he's wrong?"

"N-no, let's not. He seemed a well-meaning old codger, and I wouldn't want to hurt his feelings—if he has any. Let's go down and see what they've got for supper."

Ned's blandishments failed with the waitress, and they were established at a table presided over by a tall and very thin gentleman, whose name, as they learned presently, was Mr. Brock. There were four tables in the room, each accommodating ten boys and a member of the faculty. Diagonally across the dining-hall, the twins descried the ample Mr. Proudtree. Another table was in charge of a pleasant-faced woman who proved to be the school matron, Mrs. Wyman. Mr. Cornish, the hall master, and Mr. Barrett sat at the heads of the remaining boards.

The room was very attractive, with a fine big stone fireplace at the farther end, and broad windows on two sides. The food proved plain, but it was served in generous quantities; and notwithstanding that the twins were a bit self-conscious, they managed a very satisfactory meal.

Their fellow-students seemed to be a very decent lot. Their ages appeared to average about sixteen, and they had the clean, healthy look of boys who spent much of their time outdoors. At the table at which the twins sat, four of the boys were evidently seniors, and one was as evidently a junior. The latter looked hardly more than thirteen, though he was in reality a year older than that, and had the features and expression of a cherub. The twins concluded that he was a new boy and felt a little sorry for him. He looked much too young and innocent to face the world alone.

No one made any special effort to engage either Ned or Laurie in conversation, perhaps because the returning youths had so much to talk about among themselves. Mr. Brock ate his supper in silence, save when one of the older boys addressed him, and had a far-away and abstracted air. Laurie saw him sweeten his tea three times, and then frown in annoyance when he finally tasted it.

The boy who had guessed their awful secret at luncheon sat at the next table, and more than once Ned caught him looking across with a half-bewildered, half-frightened expression that somehow managed to convey the intelligence that, in spite of temptation, he had kept the faith. Ned finally rewarded him with a significant wink, and the youth retired in confusion behind the milk-pitcher.

When the meal was over the twins went outside and, following the example set by others, made themselves comfortable on the grass beyond the walk. Near by, two older boys were conversing earnestly, and Ned and Laurie, having exhausted their own subjects of conversation, found themselves listening.

"We've got to do it," the larger of the two was saying. "Dave's going to call a meeting of the school for Friday evening, and Mr. Wells is going to talk to them. I'll talk too. Maybe you'd better, Frank. You can tell them a funny story and get them feeling generous."

"Nothing doing, Joe. Leave me out of it. I never could talk from a platform. Anyway, it's the fellows' duty to provide money. If they don't, they won't have a team. They understand that—or they will when you tell them. There's another thing, though, Joe, that we've got to have besides money, and that's material. We've *got* to get more fellows out."

"I know. I'll tell them that, too. I'm going to put a notice up in School Hall in the morning. Mr. Cummins says there are eight new fellows entering the middle classes this year. Maybe some of them are football-players."

"Bound to be. Did you see the twins?"

"No, but Billy Emerson was telling me about them. What do they look like?"

"Not bad. Rather light-weight, though, and sort of slow. They're from Arizona or somewhere out that way, I think. You can't tell them apart, Joe."

"Think they're football stuff?"

"Search me. Might be. They're light, though. Here comes Kewpie. Gosh, he's fatter than ever! Hi, Kewpie! Come over here!"

It was Proudtree who answered the hail, descended the steps, and approached. "Hello, Joe! Hello, Frank! Well, here we are again, eh? Great to be back, isn't it? Have a good summer, Joe?"

"Fine! You?"

"Corking! I was on Dad's yacht all through August. Saw the races and everything. Bully eats, too. You understand."

"Yes," Joe Stevenson replied, "and I understand why you're about twenty pounds overweight, Kewpie! You ought to be kicked around the yard, you fat loafer. Thought you wanted to play center this fall."

"I'm going to! Listen, Joe, I'm only fourteen pounds over and I'll drop that in no time. Honest, I will. You see! Besides, it isn't all fat, either. A lot of it's good, hard muscle."

"Yes, it is! I can see you getting muscle lying around on your father's yacht! I'm off you, Kewpie. You haven't acted square. You knew mighty well that you were supposed to keep yourself fit this summer, and now look at you! You're a big fat lump!"

"Aw, say, Joe! Listen, will you?" Proudtree's gaze wandered in search of inspiration and fell on the twins. His face lighted. "Hello, you chaps!" he said. Then he leaned over and spoke to Joe. "Say, have you met the Turner brothers, Joe? One of 'em's a swell player. Played out in North Dakota or somewhere."

"Which one?" asked Joe, surreptitiously eying the twins. "Why, the—I forget: they look so much alike, you know. I think it's the one this way. Or maybe it's the other. Anyway, I'll fetch them over, eh?"

"All right, Kewpie."

Kewpie started away, paused, and spoke again. "They're—they're awfully modest chaps, Joe. You'd think from hearing them talk that they didn't know much about the game, but don't you be fooled. That's just their way. You understand."

"Oh, sure, Kewpie!" And when the latter had gone on his errand Joe smiled and, lowering his voice, said to Frank Brattle: "Kewpie's trying to put something over. I wonder what."

"Proudtree tells me one of you fellows plays football," said Joe, a minute later, when introductions had been performed and Ned and Laurie had seated themselves. "We need good players this fall. Of course, I hope you'll both come out."

"Ned's the football chap," said Laurie. "Baseball's my line."

"I don't know—" began Ned, but Laurie pinched him warningly, and he gulped and, to Kewpie's evident relief, made a fresh start. "I'm not much of a player," he said modestly, "but I'm willing to have a try at it."

Kewpie darted an "I-told-you-so" glance at Joe and Frank.

"Where do you come from, Turner?" Joe asked politely.

"Santa Lucia, California. I was in the high school there two years. Everything's quite—quite different here." Ned spoke hurriedly, as though anxious to switch the conversation from football, and Laurie smiled in wicked enjoyment. "The climate's different, you know," Ned went on desperately, "and the country and—and everything."

"I suppose so," said Frank Brattle. "What's your position, Turner?"

"Position?"

"Yes; I mean, where did you play? Behind the line, I suppose, or maybe end."

"Oh, yes, yes, behind the line. You see, I—I—"

"There aren't many fellows can play half-back the way Ned can," said Laurie, gravely. "He won't tell you so, but if you ever meet any one who saw him play against Weedon School last year—"

"Shut up!" begged Ned, almost tearfully.

Kewpie was grinning delightedly. Joe Stevenson viewed Ned with absolute affection. "Half-back, eh? Well, we can use another good half, Turner, and I hope you're the fellow. I don't know whether Kewpie told you that I'm captain this year, but I am, and I'm going to try mighty hard to captain a winning team. You look a bit light, but I dare say you're fast, and, for my part, I like them that way. Besides, we've got Mason and Boessel if we want the heavy sort. Practice starts to-morrow at four, by the way. How about your brother? Glad to have him come out, too. Even if he hasn't played, he might learn the trick. And there's next year to think of, you know."

"I think not, thanks," answered Laurie. "One football star is enough in the family."

"Well, if you change your mind, come on and have a try. Glad to have met you. See you to-morrow—er—Turner. I want to find Dave, Frank. Coming along?"

The two older boys made off toward West Hall, and as soon as they were out of hearing Ned turned indignantly on Laurie.

"You're a nice one!" he hissed. "Look at the hole you've got me in! 'Half-back'! 'Played against Weedon School'! What did you want to talk that way for? Why, those fellows think I know football!"

"Cheer up," answered his brother, grinning. "All you've got to do is bluff it through. Besides, Proudtree asked us not to let on we didn't know a football from a doughnut, and I had to say something! You acted as if you were tongue-tied!"

"Yes; that's so—you started it!" Ned turned belligerently around. "Said it would be a favor to you—" He stopped, discovering that Proudtree had silently disappeared and that he was wasting his protests on the empty air. "Huh!" he resumed after a moment of surprise, "it's a good thing he did beat it! Look here, Laurie, I'm in a beast of a mess. Yow know I can't face that captain chap to-morrow. Suppose he handed me a football and told me to kick it!"

"He won't. I've watched football practice back home. You'll stand around in a circle—"

"How the dickens can I stand in a circle?" objected Ned.

"And pass a football for a while. Then you'll try starting, and maybe fall on the ball a few times, until you're nice and lame, and after that you'll run around the track half a dozen times—"

"Oh, shut up! You make me sick! I won't do it. I'm through. I'd look fine, wouldn't I? I guess not, partner!"

"You've got to, Ned," replied Laurie calmly. "You can't back down now. The honor of the Turners is at stake! Come on up and I'll read that rules book to you. Maybe some of it'll seep in!"

After a moment of indecision Ned arose and followed silently.

CHAPTER V
IN THE PERFORMANCE OF DUTY

School began in earnest the next morning. Ned and Laurie were awakened from a deep slumber by the imperative clanging of a gong. There were hurried trips to the bath-room, and finally a descent to the recreation-room and morning prayers. Breakfast followed in the pleasant, sunlit dining-hall, and at half-past eight the twins went to their first class. There wasn't much real work performed that morning, however. Books were bought and, being again in possession of funds, Ned purchased lavishly of stationery and supplies. He had a veritable passion for patent binders, scratch-pads, blank-books, and pencils, and Laurie viewed the result of a half-hour's mad career with unconcealed concern.

"You're all wrong, Ned," he said earnestly. "We aren't opening a stationery emporium. Besides, we can't begin to compete with the office. They buy at wholesale, and—"

"Never mind the comedy. You'll be helping yourself to these things soon enough, and then you won't be so funny."

"That's the only way they'll ever get used up! Why, you've got enough truck there to last three years!"

There was one interesting annual observance that morning that the twins witnessed inadvertently. At a little after eight the fellows began to assemble in front of School Hall. Ned and Laurie, joining the throng, supposed that it was merely awaiting the half-hour, until presently there appeared at the gate a solitary youth of some fourteen years, who came up the circling drive about as joyfully as a French Royalist approaching the guillotine. Deep silence prevailed until the embarrassed and unhappy youth had conquered half of the interminable distance. Then a loud "*Hep!*" was heard, and the throng broke into a measured refrain:

"*Hep!—Hep!—Hep!—Hep!*"

This was in time to the boy's dogged steps. A look of consternation came into his face and he faltered. Then, however, he set his jaw, looked straight ahead, and came on determinedly.

"*Hep!—Hep!*"

Up the steps he passed, a disk of color in each cheek, looking neither to right nor left, and passed from sight. As he did so, the chorus changed to a good-humored laugh of approval. Ned made inquiry of a youth beside him.

"Day boy," was the explanation. "There are ten of them, you know: fellows who live in town. We always give them a welcome. That chap had spunk, but you wait and see some of them!"

Two more followed together, and, each upheld in that moment of trial by the presence of the other, passed through the ordeal with flying colors. But the twins noted that the laughing applause was lacking. After that, the remaining seven arrived almost on each other's heels and the air was filled with "*Heps!*" Some looked only surprised, others angry; but most of then grinned in a sickly, embarrassed way and went by with hanging heads.

"Sort of tough," was Ned's verdict, and Laurie agreed as they followed the last victim inside.

"It looks as if day students weren't popular," he added.

Later, though, he found that he was wrong. The boys who lived in the village were accepted without reservation, but, naturally enough, seldom attained to a full degree of intimacy with those who lived in the dormitories.

By afternoon the twins had become well shaken down into the new life, had made several superficial acquaintances, and had begun to feel at home. Of Kewpie Proudtree they had caught but fleeting glimpses, for that youth displayed a tendency to keep at a distance. As the hour of four o'clock approached, Ned became more and more worried, and his normally sunny countenance took on an expression of deep gloom. Laurie kept close at his side, fearing that courage would fail and Ned would bring disgrace to the tribe of Turner. But Laurie ought to have known better, for Ned was never what his fellows would have called a "quitter." Ned meant to see it through. His mind had retained very little of the football lore that his brother had poured into it the night before, but he had, at least, a somewhat clearer idea of the general principles of the game. He knew, for instance, that a team comprised eleven players instead of the twelve he had supposed, and that certain restrictions governed the methods by which you might wrest the ball from an opponent. Thus, you could not legally snatch it out of his arms, nor trip him up in the hope that he would drop it. Ned thought the restrictions rather silly, but accepted them.

The athletic field, known in school parlance as the play-field, was even larger than it had looked from their windows. It held two gridirons and three baseball diamonds, as well as a quarter-mile track and ten tennis-courts. There was also a picturesque and well-appointed field-house and a fairly large grand stand. To Ned's relief, most of the ninety students were in attendance, though only about forty of the number were in playing togs. Ned's idea was that among so many he might escape close observation.

He had, of course, handled a football more or less, and he was possessed of his full share of common sense. Besides, he had perhaps rather more than his share of assurance. To his own surprise, if not to Laurie's, he got through the hour and a half of practice very creditably. Seasoned candidates and novices were on the same plane to-day. There was, first of all, a talk by the coach. Mr. Mulford was a short, broad, good-humored man of about thirty, with a round and florid countenance, which possibly accounted for the nickname of "Pinky" that the school had affectionately awarded him. His real name was Stephen, and he had played guard, and played it well, for several years with Trinity College. This was his fourth season as football coach at Hillman's and his third as baseball coach. So far he had been fairly successful in both sports.

His talk was brief and earnest, although he smiled through it all. He wanted lots of material, but he didn't want any fellow to report for practice who didn't mean to do his level best and stick it out. Those who were afraid of either hard work or hard knocks had better save their time and his. Those who did report would get a fair trial and no favor. He meant to see the best team this fall that Hillman's School had ever turned out, one that would start with a rush and finish with a bang, like a rocket!

"And," he went on, "I want this team made up the way a rocket is. A rocket is filled with stars, fellows, but you don't realize it until the final burst. So we're going to put the soft pedal on individual brilliancy this year. It almost had us licked last fall, as you'll remember. This year we're going to try hard for a well-rounded team of hard workers, fellows who will interlock and gear together. It's the machine that wins, the machine of eleven parts that work all together in oil. We're going to find the eleven parts first, and after that we're going to do the oiling. All right now! Ten men to a squad. Get balls and pass in circles. Learn to hold the ball when you catch it. Glue right to it. And when you pass, put it where you want it to go. Don't think that the work is silly and unnecessary, because it isn't. A fellow who can't hold a ball when it comes to him is of no use on this team. So keep your minds right on the job and your eyes right on the ball. All right, Captain Stevenson."

At least, Ned could, to quote Laurie, "stand in a circle" and pass a football, and he did, and did it better than several others in his squad. In the same way, he could go after a trickling pigskin and catch it up without falling over himself, though it is possible that his "form" was less graceful than that of one or two of his fellows. When, later, they were formed in a line and started off by the snapping of the ball in the hands of a world-wearied youth in a faded blue sweater bearing a white H on its breast, Ned didn't show up so well, for he was almost invariably one of the last to plunge forward. The blue-sweatered youth called his attention to the fact finally in a few well-chosen words.

"You guy in the brown bloomers!" he bellowed. (Of course they weren't bloomers, but a pair of somewhat expansive golf breeches that Ned, lacking proper attire, had donned, not without misgivings, on Laurie's advice.) "Are you asleep? Put some life into it! Watch this ball, and when you see it roll, jump! You don't look like a cripple, but you surely act like one!"

Toward the end a half-dozen last-year fellows took to punting, but, to Ned's relief, no one suggested that he take a hand at it, and at half-past five or thereabouts his trials came to an end. He went out of his way, dodging behind a group on the side-line, to escape Joe Stevenson, but ran plump into Frank Brattle instead.

"Hello, Turner," Frank greeted. "How did it go?"

"All right," replied Ned, with elaborate carelessness. "Fine."

"Rather a nuisance having to go through the kindergarten stunts, isn't it?" continued the other, sympathetically. "Mulford's a great hand at what he calls the fundamentals, though. I dare say he's right, too. It's funny how easy it is to get out of the hang of things during the summer. I'm as stiff as a broom!"

"So am I," answered Ned, earnestly and truthfully. Frank smiled, nodded, and wandered on, and Ned, sighting Laurie hunched up in the grand stand, joined him. "It's a bully game, football," he sighed, as he lowered himself cautiously to a seat and listened to hear his muscles creak. "Full of beneficial effects and all that." Laurie grinned in silence. Ned felt experimentally of his back, frowned, rocked himself backward and forward twice, and looked relieved. "I guess there's nothing actually broken," he murmured, "I dare say it'll be all right soon."

"They say the first two months are the hardest," responded Laurie, comfortingly. "After that there's no sensation."

Ned nodded. "I believe it," he said feelingly. He fixed his gaze on the farther goal-post and after a minute of silence remarked:

"I'd like to catch the man who invented football!"

He turned a challenging look on his brother. Laurie blinked and for several seconds his lips moved noiselessly and there was a haunted look in his gray eyes. Then, triumphantly, he completed the couplet: "It may suit some, but it doesn't suit all!"

"Rotten!" said Ned.

"I'd like to see you do any better," answered Laurie, aggrievedly. "There isn't any proper rhyme for 'football,' anyway."

"Nor any reason for it, either. Of all—"

"Hi, you fellow!" interrupted a scandalized voice. "What are you doing up there? Have you done your two laps?"

The speaker was a lanky, red-haired man who bristled with authority and outrage.

"Two laps?" stammered Ned. "No, sir."

"Get at it, then. And beat it in when you have. Want to catch cold, do you? Sitting around without a blanket or anything like that!" The trainer shot a final disgusted look at the offender and went on.

"Gee," murmured Ned, "I thought I was done! Two laps, he said! I'll never be able to, Laurie!"

"Oh, yes, you will," was the cheerful response. "And while you're doing them you can think up a better rhyme for 'football' than I did!"

Ned looked back reproachfully as he limped to the ground and, having gained the running-track, set off at a stiff-kneed jog. Laurie's expression relented as he watched.

"Sort of tough on the kid," he muttered sympathetically. Then his face hardened again and he shook his head. "I've got to be stern with him, though!"

CHAPTER VI
NED IS FIRM

Kewpie Proudtree obeyed the shouted invitation to enter Number 16 and appeared with a countenance as innocent as that of an infant. "Hello, fellows," he said cordially, dropping into a chair with indications of exhaustion. "How do you like it as far as you've gone?"

Ned shifted in his seat at the study-table, choking back a groan, and fixed Kewpie with a baleful look. "Listen, Proudtree," he said sternly. "I've got a bone to pick with you!"

"With me?" Kewpie stared in amazement. "What have I done?"

"You've got me into a fix, that's what you've done! Didn't you ask me—us—last night not to let on to Stevenson that we—I—couldn't play football? Didn't you say it would be a favor to you? Didn't you say it would be all right and—and everything?"

"Sure! What of it?"

"Why, you crazy galoot, you must have told him that I knew all about the game! And you knew mighty well I didn't! Stevenson thinks I'm a wonder, and I don't know a touch-down from a—a forward kick!"

"Pass, not kick," corrected Kewpie, patiently. "Look here, Turner— Say, are you Ned or Laurie? Blessed if I can tell!"

"Ned," replied that youth, with much dignity.

"Guess I'll have to call you Ned, then. Can't call you both Turner. You understand. It was like this, Ned. You see, I want to stand in with Joe Stevenson. It—it's for the good of the school. If they don't play me at center this fall, who are they going to play? Well, Joe thought I—well, he seemed to think I hadn't acted just right about keeping my weight down. He—he was sort of peeved with me. So I wanted to smooth him down a bit. You understand. That's why I told him what I did."

"Well, what *did* you tell him?"

"Why, I sort of—well, it wasn't what I *said* exactly; it was what he thought I meant!"

"Proudtree, you're telling a whopper," said Ned, sternly. "And you told one to Stevenson, too, or I miss my guess."

"I only said that you were a swell football-player."

"For the love of lemons! What do you call that but a whopper?"

Kewpie looked both ashamed and distressed. He swallowed hard and glanced furtively at Laurie as though hoping for aid. But Laurie looked as unsympathetic as Ned. Kewpie sighed dolefully. "I—I suppose it was," he acknowledged. "I didn't think about that. I'm sorry, Ned, honest! I didn't mean to tell what wasn't so. I just wanted to get Joe's mind off his troubles. You understand."

"Well, you got me in a mess," grumbled Ned. "I got by all right to-day, I suppose, but what's going to happen to-morrow?"

Kewpie evidently didn't know, for he stared morosely at the floor for a long minute. Finally, "I'll go to Joe and fess up if—if you say so," he gulped.

"I think you ought to," responded Ned.

"Where's the sense in that?" demanded Laurie. "What good would it do? Proudtree did fib, but he didn't mean to. I mean he didn't do it for harm. If he goes and tells Stevenson that he fibbed, Stevenson will have it in for him harder than ever; and he will have it in for you, too, Ned. Maybe he will think it was a scheme that you and Proudtree hatched together. That's a punk idea, I say. Best thing to do is prove that Proudtree didn't fib."

"How?" asked Ned.

"Why, Proudtree—"

"There's an awful lot of that 'Proudtree' stuff," complained the visitor. "Would you mind calling me Kewpie?"

"All right. Well, Kewpie told Captain Stevenson that you are a swell player. Go ahead and be one."

"Huh, sounds easy the way you say it," scoffed Ned; "but how can I, when I don't know anything about the silly game? I wish to goodness you'd taken up football instead of me!"

"You got through to-day all right, didn't you?" asked Laurie. "Well, keep it up. Keep your eyes open and learn. You can do it. You're no fool, even if you haven't my intellect. Besides, you're the best little fakir that ever came over the range."

"You can't fake kicking a football," said Ned, scathingly.

"Look here!" exclaimed Kewpie, his round face illumined by a great idea. "Tell you what, Ned! I'll show you how to kick!"

The silence that greeted the offer might have offended a more sensitive youth, but Kewpie went on with enthusiasm. "Of course, I'm no wonder at it. I'm a little too short in the leg and, right now, I—I'm a bit heavy; but I used to kick and I know how it ought to be done. Say we have a half-hour or so at it every morning for a while?"

"Wouldn't Stevenson know what was up?" asked Ned, dubiously.

"He needn't know. We'll go over to the lot behind the grammar school. Even if he saw us, he'd think we were having some fun."

"He must have a strange idea of fun," sighed Ned. "Still, if you want to take the trouble—"

"Glad to! Besides, I owe you something for—for getting you in wrong. And I can put you wise to a lot of little things about handling a ball. We could do some passing, for instance. Wonder who's got a ball we could borrow. I'll find one somewhere. You understand. Now, what hour have you got free in the morning?"

A comparison of schedules showed that on two mornings a week the boys could meet at ten, and on two other mornings at ten-thirty. The remaining days were not accommodating, however.

"Well, even four times a week will show results," said Kewpie, cheerfully. "This is Thursday. We'll have the first lesson Saturday at ten."

"I hope they don't ask me to do any kicking before then," said Ned.

"Not likely. You'll get about the same stuff to-morrow as you had to-day. You'll get by, take my word for it. That's settled, then." Kewpie referred to an ornate gold wrist-watch. "It's after eight. You're going over to Johnny's, aren't you!"

"Johnny's?" repeated Laurie. "Oh, Doctor Hillman's! I suppose so. What's it like?"

"Oh, it isn't bad. The eats are pretty fair. Anyway, he sort of likes the fellows to go, and he's a good sort. You'll be introduced to the faculty and their wives, if they have any, and meet a lot of fellows whose names you'll forget the next minute. Take my advice and sort of work in toward the dining-room. Last year, the harlequin ice-cream gave out before I could get to the table." Kewpie sighed. "Tabby has bully cake, too, and I'm off of cake. Isn't that rotten luck?"

"Awful!" laughed Ned. "You going over now?"

"Yes. Come on and I'll introduce you to some of the fellows you ought to know. I'll wash my dirty paws and meet you in two minutes."

The principal's reception proved rather enjoyable. The "eats" were excellent and, under Kewpie's guidance, the twins reached the long table in the dining-room well in advance of the crowd. As Laurie remarked afterward, it was worth the amount of trouble involved just to watch Kewpie's mouth water as he gazed soulfully at the chocolate layer-cake. To his credit be it narrated that he manfully resisted it. Besides consuming much delectable food, the twins were impressively introduced by their guide to a number of their fellow-students, the introduction being prefaced in each case by a sort of biographical note, as: "There's Dan Whipple. The tall fellow with the trick collar, talking to Mrs. Wells. Rows stroke on the crew. Senior class president. Honor man last year. President of Attic, too. Good chap to know. Come on." In such manner they met at least a half-dozen school notables, most of whom were extremely affable to the new boys. Sometimes, to be sure, the twins had a suspicion that Kewpie was pretending a closer intimacy with a notable than in fact existed, but he always "got away with it."

The only fly in the ointment of the evening's enjoyment occurred when Kewpie mischievously introduced them to Mrs. Pennington, the wife of the Greek and Latin instructor, and sneaked away. Mrs. Pennington was tall and extremely thin, and viewed the world through a pair of tortoise-shell spectacles. She had a high voice and what Ned termed a "very Lake Superior" manner, and, since she confined her conversation to the benefits to be derived from an earnest study of the Latin poets, philosophers, and historians, the twins were not happy. Fortunately, very little was demanded from them conversationally, Mrs. Pennington being quite competent to do all the talking. But, unfortunately, she gave them no chance to get away. Ned descried Kewpie grinning heartlessly from the doorway and rewarded him with a terrific and threatening scowl. Kewpie, however, waved blandly and faded into the night. Release came to them at last and they scurried away, neglecting, in their hurried departure, to say good night either to the doctor or Miss Tabitha, a breach of etiquette which probably passed unnoted by the hosts. Back in East Hall, the twins hammered loudly at Number 15, but Kewpie was either absent or discreet. At any rate, there was no response, and revenge had to be postponed.

To Laurie's surprise, a notice on the bulletin-board in the corridor of School Hall the following morning announced that autumn baseball practice would begin that afternoon. He had supposed that his hour to offer himself on the altar of school patriotism would not arrive until the next spring; and later, when he strode down Walnut Street with Ned, in search of football togs for the latter, he broached the subject diplomatically.

"Funny idea to have baseball practice this time of year, I think," he remarked carelessly. "Not much good in it. A fellow would forget anything he learned by next April."

"Didn't know they did," replied Ned, uninterestedly. "Who told you that?"

"Oh, there was a notice on the board in School Hall. Don't believe many fellows go out in the fall."

"Thought baseball was a spring and summer game. Still, I dare say you can play it just as well now. Seems to me I've heard of having spring football practice, haven't you?"

"I dare say. Crazy scheme, though, playing games out of season."

"Ye-es." Ned went on thoughtfully a moment Then he shot a suspicious glance at his brother. "You going out?" he demanded.

"N-no, I don't think so," answered Laurie, lightly. "There's that building we had the bet on the other day. We never did find out—"

"Never you mind about that building," interrupted Ned, severely. "I'm on to you, partner. You're trying to renege on baseball. Well, it doesn't go! You're a baseball hero and you've got to get busy!"

"Aw, Ned, have a heart! There's plenty of time—"

"No, sir, by jiminy! You got me slaving for the dear old school, now you do your bit!"

"Yes, but it isn't fair to start the baseball season in September. You know it isn't."

"Cut out the alibis! You can get some baseball togs right now. Good thing you spoke of it. What'll you need?"

"All I need is kindness," wailed Laurie. "Ned, I don't want to be a hero! I don't want to save the dear old school from defeat in the ninth inning! I—I—"

"You're going to do as you agreed to," answered Ned, grimly. "Remember that the honor of the Turners is at stake!"

Laurie sighed deeply. Then, "You speak of honor! Say no more. I yield," he declaimed dramatically.

"You bet you do," answered Ned, unhesitatingly. "You for the baseball field!"

CHAPTER VII
HIGH SCHOOL ACCEPTS DEFEAT

A week passed, and the twins began to feel like old residents. They had ceased being "the Turner twins" to acquaintances, although others still referred to them so, and their novelty had so far worn off that they could enter a classroom or walk side by side across the yard without being conscious of the rapt, almost incredulous stares of the beholders. To merely casual acquaintances they were known as Ned and Laurie; to a few friends they had become Nid and Nod. Kewpie was responsible for that. He had corrupted "Ned" into "Nid," after which it was impossible for Laurie to be anything but "Nod." Laurie had demurred for a time, demanding to be informed who Nod had been. Kewpie couldn't tell him, being of the hazy belief that Nid and Nod were brothers in some fairy story he had once read, but he earnestly assured Laurie that both had been most upright and wholly estimable persons. Anyhow, Laurie's objections wouldn't have accomplished much, for others had been prompt to adopt the nicknames and all the protests in the world wouldn't have caused them to drop them. These others weren't many in number, however: Kewpie and Thurman Kendrick and Lee Murdock and George Watson about made up the list of them at this time.

Kendrick was Kewpie's room-mate, a smallish, black-haired, very earnest youth of sixteen, which age was also Kewpie's. Thurman was familiarly known as "Hop," although the twins never learned why. He was a candidate for quarter-back on the eleven and took his task very seriously. Lee Murdock was one of the baseball crowd, and Laurie had scraped acquaintance with him on the diamond during a practice game. The word "scraped" is used advisedly, for Laurie, in sliding to second base, had spiked much of the skin from Lee's ankle. Of such incidents are friendships formed! Lee was two years older than Laurie, a big, rather raw-boned fellow with a mop of ash-colored hair and very bright blue eyes.

George Watson was sixteen, an upper middler, and, as Laurie frequently assured him, no fit associate for a respectable fellow. To the latter assertion George cheerfully agreed, adding that he always avoided such. He came from Wyoming and had brought with him a breeziness of manner that his acquaintances, rightly or wrongly, described as "wild and woolly." Of the four, Kewpie and George were more often found in company with the twins.

There had been four lessons in kicking on an open lot behind the grammar school, two short blocks away, and while Ned had not yet mastered the gentle art of hurtling a football through the air, Kewpie was enthusiastic about his pupil's progress. "Why, geewhillikins, Nid," he broke forth after the fourth session, "you're a born kicker! Honest you are! You've got a corking swing and a lot of drive. You—you've got real *form*, that's what you've got. You understand. And you certainly do learn! Of course, you haven't got it all from me, because you've been punting in practice two or three times, but I take some of the credit."

"You've got a right to," responded Ned. "You've taught me a lot more than I've learned on the field. Gee, if it hadn't been for you I'd been afraid even to try a punt over there! You ought to see the puzzled way that Pope looks at me sometimes. He can't seem to make me out, because, I suppose, Joe Stevenson told him I was a crackajack. Yesterday he said, 'You get good distance, Turner, and your direction isn't bad, but you never punt twice the same way!'"

"Well, you don't," laughed Kewpie. "But you'll get over that just as soon as I can get it into your thick head that the right way's the best and there's only one right!"

"I know," said Ned, humbly. "I mean to do the way you say, but I sort of forget."

"That's because you try to think of too many things at once. Stop thinking about your leg and just remember the ball and keep your eyes on it until it's in the air. That's the secret, Nid. I heard Joe telling Pinky the other day that you'd ought to shape up well for next year."

"Next year!" exclaimed Ned, dubiously. "Gee! mean to tell me I'm going through all this work for next year?"

"Well, you might get a place this year, for all you know," replied Kewpie, soothingly. "Just keep on coming, Nid. If you could only—well, if you had just a bit more *speed* now, got started quicker, you know, Pinky would have you on the second squad in no time, I believe. You're all right after you get started, but—you understand."

"I do the best I know how," sighed Ned. "I suppose I am slow on the get-away, though. Corson is always calling me down about it. Oh, well, what do I care? I don't own it."

"I'd like to see you make good, though," said Kewpie. "Besides, remember the honor of the Turners!"

Ned laughed. "Laurie will look after that. He's doing great things in baseball, if you believe him, and it wouldn't be right for us to capture all the athletic honors."

"You make me weary!" grunted Kewpie. "Say, don't you California chaps ever have any pep?"

"California, old scout, is famous for its pep. We grow it for market out there. Why, I've seen a hundred acres planted to it!"

"You have, eh? Well, it's a big shame you didn't bring a sprig of it East with you, you lazy lummox! Some day I'm going to drop a cockle-burr down your back and see if you don't show some action!"

Hillman's started her season on the following Saturday with Orstead High School. As neither team had seen much practice, the contest didn't show a very high grade of football. The teams played four ten-minute quarters, consuming a good two hours of elapsed time in doing it, their members spending many precious moments prone on the turf. The weather was miserably warm for football and the players were still pretty soft.

Kewpie derived great satisfaction from the subsequent discovery that he had dropped three quarter pounds and was within a mere seven pounds of his desired weight. Had he played the game through instead of yielding the center position to Holmes at the beginning of the last half, he might have reached his goal that afternoon. Ned and Laurie wounded him deeply by declaring that there was no apparent improvement in his appearance.

Ned saw the game from the substitutes' bench, and Laurie from the stand. High School turned out a full attendance and, since Hillman's was outnumbered two to one, "O. H. S." colors and cheers predominated. Laurie sat with Lee Murdock, who, as a baseball enthusiast, professed a great scorn of football. (There was no practice on the diamond that afternoon.) Lee amused himself by making ridiculous comments in a voice audible for many yards around.

"That's piffle!" he declared on one occasion, when the ground was strewn with tired, panting players. "The umpire said, 'Third down,' but if they aren't three quarters down, I'll treat the crowd! The trouble with those fellows is that they didn't get enough sleep last night. Any one can see that. Why, I can hear that big chap snoring 'way over here!" Again, "That brother of yours is playing better than any of them," he asserted.

"Ned? Why, he isn't in! He's on the bench down there."

"Sure! That's what I mean. You don't see him grabbing the ball away from Brattle and losing two or three yards at a time. No, sir; he just sits right there, half asleep, and makes High School *work* for the game. Every time he doesn't take the ball, Nod, he saves us three or four yards. He's a hero, that's what he is. If Mulford would get all the rest of them back on the bench, we might win."

"You're crazy," laughed Laurie.

During the intermission, Laurie's wandering gaze fell on two girls a dozen seats away. One, whom he had never seen before, displayed a cherry-and-black pennant and belonged unmistakably to the high school cohort. She was a rather jolly-looking girl, Laurie decided, with a good deal of straw-colored hair and a pink-and-white skin. Her companion was evidently divided as to allegiance, for she had a cherry-and-black ribbon pinned on the front of her dress and wore a dark-blue silken arm-band. For a moment Laurie wondered why she looked familiar to him. Then he recognized her as Polly Deane. The two girls appeared to be alone, although some boys in the row behind were talking to them.

So far, the twins had not been back to the little shop on Pine Street, but Laurie resolved now that he would drop around there very soon and pay his bill before his money was gone. After paying the school bill for the first half-year, he and Ned had shared slightly more than twenty dollars, but since then there had been many expenses. They had each had to purchase playing togs and stationery, and, finally, had donated two dollars apiece to the football fund at the mass-meeting Friday night of the week before.

Viewed from a financial standpoint, that meeting hadn't been a great success, and it was no secret that, unless more money was forthcoming, the team would be obliged to cancel at least one of its away-from-home games. But it had resulted in bringing out a big field of candidates, and there had been a lot of enthusiasm. The next day, viewing his reduced exchequer, Laurie had ruefully observed that he guessed a dollar would have been enough to give, but Ned had called him a "piker" and a "tight-wad" and other scornful things. Yesterday Ned had borrowed half a dollar, which was more than a fourth of Laurie's remaining cash; and the first of October was still a week distant. Realizing the latter fact, Laurie changed his mind about settling his account at the Widow Deane's. But, he reflected, with another friendly glance in Polly's direction, it wouldn't be right to withhold his trade from the store. And he wasn't anywhere near the limit of indebtedness yet!

Two listless periods followed the intermission, the only inspiring incident coming when, near the end of the third quarter, Pope, Hillman's full-back, foiled in his attempt to get a forward pass away, smashed past the enemy and around his left end for a run that placed the pigskin six yards short of the last white line. From there the home team managed to push its way to a touch-down, the third and last score of the day. The final figures were 10 to 7 in Hillman's favor, and neither side was very proud of the outcome.

Ned returned to Number 16 half an hour later in a most critical frame of mind, and spent ten minutes explaining to Laurie just when and how the school team had failed. At last Laurie interrupted him to ask, "Have you told this to Mr. Mulford, Ned?"

"Mr. Mulford? Why—oh, go to the dickens!"

"Seems to me he ought to know," said Laurie, gravely.

"That's all right. You can be sarcastic if you like, but I'm talking horse-sense. You see a lot of things from the bench that you don't see from the stand. Besides, you've got to know football to understand it. Now you take—"

"I beg your pardon! Did you say anything about understanding football?"

"Well, I understand a lot more about it than you do," replied the other, warmly. "I've been playing it a week, haven't I?"

"Sure, but I'll bet you don't know how much a safety counts!"

"I don't need to. That's up to the referee. But I know some football, just the same. And I punted forty-seven yards yesterday, too!"

"In how many punts?" inquired Laurie, innocently.

Ned threw a book at him and the subject was closed.

In his own line, baseball, Laurie was not setting the world on fire. He was gaining a familiarity with the position of center fielder on the scrub nine, and batting practice was at least not doing him any harm. But he certainly had displayed no remarkable ability; and if Ned had gained a notion to the contrary, it was merely because it pleased Laurie to fool him with accounts of imaginary incidents in which he, Laurie, had shone most brilliantly. As Ned knew even less about baseball than he had known of football, almost any fairy-tale "went" with him, and Laurie derived much amusement thereby; decidedly more, in fact, than he derived from playing!

On Monday morning Laurie dragged Ned over to the Widow Deane's for ginger-ale, professing a painful thirst. The Widow greeted them pleasantly, recalling their names, and provided them with the requested beverage. Laurie's thirst seemed to have passed, for he had difficulty in consuming his portion. When, presently, he asked politely about Polly, it developed that that young lady was quite well enough to attend high school as usual. Laurie said, "Oh!" and silently promised himself that the next time he got thirsty it would be in the afternoon. Ned ate two doughnuts and was hesitating over raspberry tarts when Laurie dragged him away. "Can't you think of anything but eating?" demanded the latter, disgustedly. Ned only blinked.

"Ginger-ale always makes me hungry," he explained calmly.

Two days later, the twins awoke to cloudy skies, and by mid-forenoon a lazy drizzle was falling, which later turned to a downright tempest of wind and rain. At four the baseball candidates scooted to the field-house for cover, although, peering forth through a drenched window, Laurie discerned the football-players still at work. Lee Murdock said he guessed the equinoctial storm had come, and that if it had there'd be no practice for a couple of days. Laurie tried to look broken-hearted and failed dismally. Taking advantage of a lull in the downpour, he and Lee, with many of the others, set forth for school. They were still far short of the gymnasium, however, when the torrent began again, and it was a wet, bedraggled, and breathless crowd that presently pushed through the door.

George Watson, who had been playing tennis before the rain started, was philosophically regarding a pair of "unshrinkable" flannel trousers which, so he declared, had already receded an inch at the bottoms. It was George who suggested that, after changing to dry clothing, they go over to the Widow's and have ice-cream at his expense. Not possessing a rain-coat of his own, Laurie invaded Number 15 and borrowed Kewpie's. It was many sizes too large, but it answered. The Widow's was full when he and George and Lee got there, and the pastry counter looked as though it had been visited by an invading army. There was still ice-cream, though, and the three squeezed into a corner and became absorbedly silent for a space.

Polly was helping her mother, and Laurie exchanged greetings with her, but she was far too busy for conversation. Lee treated to a second round of ice-cream, and afterward Laurie bought a bag of old-fashioned chocolates. He hoped Polly would wait on him, but it was Polly's mother who did so and asked after his brother as she filled the paper sack.

"I do hope you're looking after him and that he hasn't eaten those raspberry tarts yet," she said pleasantly.

"Yes'm," said Laurie. "I mean, he hasn't." He thought it surprising that the Widow Deane was able to tell them apart. Even Kewpie and George frequently made mistakes.

It was still pouring when they went out again, and they hurried up the street and around the corner into School Park, their progress somewhat delayed by the fact that Laurie had placed the bag of candy in an outside pocket of Kewpie's capacious rain-coat and that all three had difficulty in finding it. Lee had just popped a big chocolate into his mouth and George was fumbling into the moist bag when the clouds opened suddenly and such a deluge fell as made them gasp. In distance they were but a long block from school; but with the rain descending on them as though poured from a million buckets, their thought was of immediate shelter.

"Wow!" yelped Lee. "Let's get out of this! Here's a house. Come on!"

There was an opening in a high hedge, and a short brick walk from which the drops were rebounding knee-high, and, seen dimly through the deluge, a porch at the end of it. They reached it in what Laurie called three leaps and a jump, and, under shelter of the roof, drew breath and looked back into the gray welter. The park was invisible, and even the high lilac hedge was only a blurred shape. Lee had to shout to make himself heard above the rain.

"Wonder who lives here," he said. "I don't remember this house."

"Sure you do!" said George. "This is the Coventry house. We're on the side porch."

"Oh!" Lee gazed doubtfully into the rain. "Well, anyway, it'll do. Gee, my trousers are soaked to the knees! How long do you suppose this will keep up?"

"You said for two days," answered Laurie, cheerfully, trying to dry his neck with a moist handkerchief.

"I mean this shower, you chump!"

"Call this a shower? What's a cloud-burst like in this part of the country, then?"

"We don't have such things," answered George, who was peering through a side-light into the dim interior. "Say, I thought this place was empty," he continued. "I can see chairs and a table in there."

"No; some one rented it this fall," said Lee. "I noticed the other day that the front door was open and the grass had been cut. I wouldn't want to live in the place, though."

"Why?" inquired Laurie.

But, before any answer came, the door was suddenly opened within a few inches of George's nose and a voice said:

"You fellows had better come inside until it's over."

CHAPTER VIII
IN THE MISER'S HOUSE

The invitation came from a boy of about sixteen, a slim, eminently attractive chap, who smiled persuasively through the aperture. Laurie knew that he had seen him somewhere, but it was not until they had followed, somewhat protestingly, into a hallway and from there into a large and shadowy drawing-room that he recognized him as one of the day pupils. Lee, it seemed, knew him slightly and called him by name.

"We oughtn't to come in here," Lee apologized. "We're soaking wet, Starling."

"It doesn't matter," answered their host. "Wait till I find a match and we'll have a fire here."

"Don't bother, please," George protested. "We're going right on in a minute."

"Might as well get dry a bit first. The fire's all laid." The boy held a match at the grate and in a moment the wood was snapping merrily. "Pull up some chairs, fellows. Here, try this. Some rain, isn't it?"

"Rather," agreed Lee. "By the way, do you know Turner? And Watson?" The three boys shook hands. "I didn't know you lived here," Lee continued. "Saw the house had been taken, but didn't know who had it. Corking big place, isn't it?"

Starling laughed. "It's big all right, but it's not so corking. Let me have that rain-coat, Turner. The rooms are so frightfully huge that you get lost in them! I have the bedroom above this, and the first morning I woke up in it I thought I was in the Sahara Desert! This was the only place we could find, though, that was for rent, and we had to take it. Dad came here on short notice and we didn't have much time to look around. Pull up closer to the fire, Watson, and get your feet dry. I've got some slippers upstairs if you want to take your shoes off."

"No, thanks. I guess the wet didn't get through. I've seen you over at school, haven't I?"

"Yes, I'm a day boy; one of the 'Hep, heps!'"

Lee grinned. "Sort of a mean trick, that, Starling, but they always do it every year."

"Wish I'd known about it beforehand. I'd have sneaked over a fence and through a window. It was fierce! I was the last fellow to get in this fall. Dad made application in August, and some fellow who had entered in the spring changed his mind; otherwise I'd have had to go to the high school."

"That would have been an awful fate," said George, gravely.

"Oh, I wouldn't have minded. I like Hillman's, though. Do any of you chaps play tennis?"

"I try to," answered George.

"Wish you'd give me a game some day. Tennis is about the only thing I know much about, and I saw some dandy courts over at the field."

"Glad to," George assured him. "Any day you like, Starling. I'm not much of a player, though, so don't expect a lot."

"Guess you're good enough to handle me," laughed the other. "I like it better than I can play it. How about to-morrow afternoon?"

"Suits me," answered George. "Three-thirty?"

"Fine! I'm going to get Dad to build a court in the yard here, if I can. There's lots of room, but there's a tumble-down old grape-arbor right in the middle."

"Yes, there's surely room enough," agreed Lee. "We used to come over here last fall and get pears—there's a dandy seckel tree back there. I'd say there was room for two or three courts if some of the trees were cut down."

"What could he do with three of them?" asked Laurie.

"I suppose we'd have to get the owner's permission to even take that rickety old arbor down," Starling said.

"I thought the owner was dead," Lee observed.

George chuckled. "If he was dead he wouldn't be the owner, you simple! Old Coventry died three or four years ago, but somebody owns the place, of course. If what they tell of the old chap is true, it must have broken his heart to know he couldn't take the place with him! Maybe he took his money with him, though. Anyway, the story goes that he had slathers of it, and they could only find a couple of thousands when he died."

"What was he, a miser?" asked Starling.

"Yes, one of the sort you read about in the stories. Lived here all alone for years and years with only a negro servant. They say you could never see a light in the place at night, and he never went off the front porch more than a couple of times a year. Then a carriage came for him and he got in and went down to the boat. He didn't use the train because it cost too much. Of course, when he died, folks expected to find that he had left a mint of money; but all any one could discover was about two thousand dollars in one of the banks here—that, and this property. The heirs, whoever they were, pretty near tore the insides out of the house, they say, looking for coin, but they didn't get any thing."

"And at night the old codger's ghost walks around," added Lee; "and if you follow him, he'll take you to the place the money's hidden."

"Honest?" exclaimed Starling, joyfully. "Gosh, that's great! I always wanted to live in a house with a ghost."

"I'm sorry, then," said George, "for I just made that part up."

"*You* did?" Lee looked incredulous. "Where do you come in? I've heard that ever since I came here."

"No, sir; you may have heard the rest of the story, but not the part about the ghost. I wrote the yarn up in my junior year for an English comp., and tacked on the ghost feature as a sort of added climax. Got good marks, too, and the Orstead paper published the thing. I'll show it to you, if you like."

Lee looked unconvinced still, and Starling disappointed. "Well, it's a good story, anyway, and makes the place more interesting. Some day I'll have a look myself for the hidden millions."

"Guess the old chap never had that much," said George. "Thirty or forty thousand is about what he was supposed to have salted away."

"Scarcely worth bothering about," observed Laurie, with a yawn.

"But look here, what became of the servant?" asked Starling. "Maybe he got the dough and made off with it."

"Lots of folks thought that," replied George; "but the theory didn't pan out for a cent. The negro stuck around here for quite a while and then ambled off somewhere. He claimed that old Coventry died owing him a month's wages, and tried to get some one to pay him, but I guess he never got any of it, if it was really owing."

"Where did he go to?" asked Starling.

"I don't know. New York City, I think."

"I'll bet he either had the money or knew where it was," declared Starling, with conviction. "Don't you see, fellows, he did just what any one would do in his case? He stuck around so he wouldn't be suspected. If he'd gone right off, folks would have said he was trying to avoid being asked about the money. And then he faked up the yarn about the old gentleman owing him wages. A first-class detective would have got trace of the coin, I'll wager!"

"You've been reading *Sherlock Holmes*," laughed Lee. "Why don't you follow up your clue, find the negro, and restore the lost wealth to the starving heirs?"

"Huh! If he did get the money, he's where even *Sherlock Holmes* wouldn't find him by this time. Some one should have followed the fellow and kept watch on him right then. How old was he, Watson?"

"About fifty, I guess. They say he had white whiskers, anyway. Oh, he didn't know any more than he said he did. He was all right. He had been with old Coventry for years and years, one of those old-time family servants, you know, honest and faithful. Why, he went on something fierce when the old chap died!"

"Say, how much of this guff is real and how much of it is English composition?" asked Lee, suspiciously. "How do you know the negro took on when the old codger died? You weren't here."

"Maybe I heard it," replied George, grinning.

"Yes, and maybe you just made it up, like the stuff about the ghost," Lee retorted sarcastically. "I've heard the yarn two or three times, but I never heard that the negro had white whiskers or that he went into mourning!"

"It's a fact, though," declared the other, warmly. "I prepared mighty well on that comp.; talked with half a dozen persons who knew the story. Got most of the stuff from the Widow Deane, though. Old Coventry had been dead only about two years then and folks were still talking about him. The Widow doesn't think the old chap had nearly as much money as he was supposed to have."

"She has the little store around on the back street?" asked Starling.

"Yes. She took that as her share."

"Her share of what?" demanded Lee.

"Why, of the estate. Old Coventry owned the whole half-block right through from Walnut Street to Pine. She rented that house from him until he died; paid a good stiff price, too; and then, when the estate was finally settled, she took it as her share, although she had to pay the other heirs something because they claimed that it was worth more than she had a right to."

"Look here," said Lee, "do you mean that the Widow Deane was one of old Coventry's heirs?"

"Of course! Didn't you know it? She was a half-sister. She lived over in New Jersey, she told me, until her husband died. Then she wrote to old Coventry, asking him to help her because she didn't have much money, and he invited her to come here. She thought he meant to give her a home with him; but when she got here, the best he would do was rent her that little house around on Pine Street and stock it up for her as a store. Then he built a fence between the two places. It used to be open right through."

"Gee, you certainly know a lot of ancient history!" marveled Lee.

"I believe in being thorough," laughed George. "When I tackle a subject I get a fall out of it."

"So when I trail the murderer—I mean the thief," reflected Starling, "I'll be doing the old lady back there a good turn, won't I?"

"Surest thing you know!" agreed George.

"And she needs the money, I guess. I don't believe she makes a fortune out of that emporium. And that daughter of hers is a nice kid, too."

"How many other heirs are there to share in the money when Starling finds it?" asked Laurie.

"I don't know. Quite a bunch, I believe. The old chap wasn't married, and the heirs are nephews and nieces and things like that. The Widow's the only one living around here, though."

"Well, when I do find it," laughed Starling, "I'll keep it quiet and hand it all over to the Widow."

"He wants to make a hit with Polly," said Lee. "He's a fox."

"I've never seen her," Starling denied.

"Well, she's a mighty pretty girl," George avowed. "If you don't believe me, ask Nod."

Laurie looked intensely innocent and very surprised. "Why me?" he asked blandly.

George shook his head, grinning. "You can't get away with it, son! Think I didn't see you making love to the old lady this afternoon?"

"Well," Laurie laughed, "I thought it was Polly you spoke of."

"Sure, but she was busy waiting on a bunch of juniors and so you made up to the Widow. We saw you smirking and talking sweet to her, didn't we, Lee? Butter wouldn't have melted in the dear lamb's mouth. And I thought the old lady seemed rather taken with him, too; didn't you, Lee?"

"Rather! It was positively sickening! Talk about foxes—"

"Oh, dry up and blow away!" muttered Laurie. "Say, the rain's stopped now—pretty nearly."

"Wants to get away from the embarrassing subject," George confided to Starling. "Well, I never desert a pal, Nod. Come on, we'll trot along. Much obliged for taking us in, Starling. Hope we haven't ruined your rug. Half-past three to-morrow, if the courts are dry. I'll meet you in School Hall."

"Glad to have you drop around at my room some time," said Lee. "I'm in West; Number 7."

"Same here," added Laurie; "16 East Hall. Thanks, Starling."

"You're welcome. Come in again, fellows. When I get that tennis-court fixed up, we'll have some fun here. You needn't wait for that, though. I'd like you to meet my father and aunt. No one's at home just now. I say, better take a couple of umbrellas."

"Not worth it, thanks," answered Lee. "After that deluge, this is just an April shower. So long!"

Lee's statement wasn't much of an exaggeration, and the three continued their way to the school unhurriedly. George remarked gloomily that it didn't look awfully promising for tennis on the morrow, adding: "I'll bet that chap's a corking good player, too."

"Maybe you'll learn a little about the game from him," said Laurie, sweetly. "How old do you say he is?"

"Starling? Oh, seventeen, maybe. He's in upper middle."

"Sixteen, more likely," said George. "He seems a decent sort, eh? How did you come to know him?"

"I didn't really know him. He's in some of my classes and we've spoken a couple of times. Rather a—an interesting kind of chap. Wonder what his father does here. Funny place for him to come to. He spoke of an aunt, but didn't say anything about a mother. Guess she's dead. Auntie probably keeps house for them."

As they entered the gate George chuckled and Laurie asked, "What's your trouble, Old-Timer!"

"I was just thinking what a joke it would be if Starling took that stuff seriously about the hidden money and began to hack away the woodwork and dig up the cellar floor!"

"Why, wasn't it true?"

"Sure! At least, as true as anything is that folks tell. You know, Nod, after being repeated a couple of hundred times a story sort of grows."

Lee grunted. "After some smart Aleck has written it up as an English comp. its own mother wouldn't know it! The real joke would be for Starling to wreck the woodwork and find the money!"

"No, that wouldn't be a joke," said George, "that would be a movie! Come on! It's starting again! Last man in East buys the sodas! Come on, Lee!"

Lee and Laurie ran a dead heat, and all the way to George's room, on the second floor, each sought to shift to the other the responsibility of providing the soda-water for the trio. In the end, George appointed himself referee and halved the responsibility between them.

When, twenty minutes later, Laurie climbed onward to Number 16, he found a very disgruntled Ned curled up in the window-seat, which was now plentifully supplied with cushions. "Where've you been all the afternoon?" he demanded aggrievedly.

"Many places," replied Laurie, cheerfully. "Why the grouch?"

"You'd have a grouch, I reckon, if you'd messed around with a soggy football for almost two hours in a cloud-burst!"

"Did you—er—get wet?"

"Oh, no, I didn't get wet! I carried an umbrella all the time, you silly toad! Or maybe you think they roofed the gridiron over for us?"

"Well, I got sort of water-logged myself, and don't you let any one tell you any different! Wait till I return this rain-coat and I'll tell you about it."

"I've got troubles enough of my own," grumbled Ned, as Laurie crossed the corridor.

Kewpie wasn't in when the borrowed garment was returned, but Hop Kendrick was, and Hop said it was quite all right, that Ned was welcome to anything of Kewpie's at any time, and please just stick it in the closet or somewhere. And Laurie thanked him gratefully and placed the rain-coat, which wasn't very wet now, where he had found it. And the incident would have ended then and there if it hadn't started in to rain cats and dogs again after supper and if Kewpie hadn't taken it into his head to pay a visit to a fellow in West Hall. Which is introductory to the fact that at eight o'clock that evening, while Ned and Laurie were conscientiously absorbed in preparing to-morrow's Latin, a large and irate youth appeared at the door of Number 16 with murder in his eyes and what appeared to be gore on his hands!

"That's a swell way to return a fellow's coat!" he accused.

He brandished one gory hand dramatically, and with the other exhumed from a pocket of the garment a moist and shapeless mass of brown paper and chocolate creams. "Look at this!" he exhorted. "It—it's all over me! The pocket's a regular glue-pot! Ugh!"

Laurie looked and his shoulders heaved.

"Oh, Kewpie!" he gurgled, contrition—or something—quite overmastering him. "I'm s-s-so s-s-sorry!"

Kewpie regarded him scathingly a moment, while syrupy globules detached themselves from the exhibit and ran along his wrist. Finally he exploded: "Sorry! Yes, you are!"

Whereupon the door closed behind him with an indignant crash, and Laurie, unable longer to contain his sorrow, dropped his head on his books and gave way to it unrestrainedly.

CHAPTER IX
LAURIE HEARS NEWS

October arrived with the first touch of cooler weather, and the football candidates, who had panted and perspired under summer conditions for a fortnight, took heart. Among these was Ned. Laurie, who at first had had to alternate sympathy and severity in order to keep his brother's courage to the sticking-point, now found that his encouragement was no longer needed. Ned was quite as much in earnest as any fellow who wore canvas. Probably he was not destined ever to become a mighty player, for he seemed to lack that quality which coaches, unable to describe, call football instinct. But he had made progress—surprising progress when it is considered that he had known virtually nothing of the game two weeks before.

Laurie, whose afternoons were still absorbed by baseball, viewed Ned's efforts as something of a joke, much to the latter's chagrin, and continued to do so until a chance conversation with Thurman Kendrick opened his eyes. Hop had come across one forenoon to borrow some notes and had tarried a moment to talk. In those days, when Hop talked he talked of just one subject, and that subject was football, and he introduced it to-day.

"We've got to do better to-morrow than we did last week," he said earnestly, "or we'll get licked hard. Cole's was fairly easy, but Highland is a tough customer. Our trouble so far has been slowness, and Highland's as fast as they make them. Somehow, Mulford doesn't seem able to get any pep into our bunch. The line isn't so bad, but the back field's like cold glue."

"That's up to the quarter, isn't it?" asked Laurie, anxious to prove himself not absolutely ignorant of the subject.

"Yes, partly; but it's up to the coach first. If the backs aren't used to working fast, the quarter can't make them. Frank Brattle's a good quarter, Nod. I sort of wish he wasn't so good!"

"Meaning you'd have a better chance of swiping his job?" smiled Laurie.

"Oh, I'll never do that; but if he wasn't so good I'd get in more often. The best I can hope for this year is to get in for maybe a full period in the Farview game. Anyway, I'll get my letter, and maybe next year I'll land in the position. Frank's a senior, you know."

"Is he? I haven't seen much practice so far. Baseball keeps me pretty busy."

"How are you getting on?"

"Slow, I'm afraid. Anyway, you could easily tell Babe Ruth and me apart!"

"I guess you're doing better than you let on," said Hop. "If you're as good at baseball as your brother is at football, you'll do."

"I guess I am," laughed Laurie; "just about!"

"Well, Nid is surely coming fast," replied Hop, gravely. "He's been doing some nice work the last few days."

Laurie stared. "Say, what are you doing, Hop? Stringing me?" he demanded.

"Stringing you?" Hop looked puzzled. "Why, no. How do you mean?"

"About Ned. Do you mean that he's really playing football?"

"Why, of course I do. Didn't you know it?"

Laurie shook his head. "He's been telling me a lot of stuff, but I thought he was just talking, the way I've been, to sort of keep his courage up."

"Nonsense! Nid's doing mighty well. I don't know how much experience he's had; some ways he acts sort of green; but he's got Mason worried, I guess. If he had another fifteen pounds he'd make the team sure. As it is, I wouldn't be surprised to see him play a whole lot this fall. You see, he's a pretty good punter, Nod, and yesterday he blossomed out as a drop-kicker, too. Landed the ball over from about the thirty yards and from a hard angle. Mason doesn't do any kicking, and it's no bad thing to have a fellow in the back field who can help Pope out in a pinch. It's his kicking ability that'll get him on if anything does."

"I see," said Laurie, thoughtfully. "Well, I'm mighty glad. To tell the truth, Hop, Ned hasn't had an awful lot of experience. He's had to bluff a good deal."

"I suspected something of the sort from seeing him work the first week or so. And then Kewpie said something that sort of lined up with the idea. Well, he's working hard and he's making good. Much obliged for these, Nod. I'll fetch them back in ten minutes."

When Kendrick had taken his departure Laurie stared thoughtfully for a minute into space. Finally he shook his head and smiled. "Good old Ned!" he murmured. "I'm sorry I ragged him so. Gee, I'll have to buckle down to my own job or he'll leave me at the post!"

After practice that afternoon, Laurie and Lee picked up George and Bob Starling at the tennis-courts, and, after changing into "cits," went around to the doctor's porch and joined a dozen other lads who were engaged in drinking Miss Tabitha's weak tea and eating her soul-satisfying layer-cake. After a half-hour of batting and fielding practice and a five-inning game between the first team and the scrubs, Laurie was in a most receptive mood as far as refreshments were concerned. Miss Tabitha made an ideal hostess, for she left conversation to the guests and occupied herself in seeing that cups and plates were kept filled. No one had yet discovered the number of helpings of cake that constituted Miss Tabitha's limit of hospitality, and there was a story of a junior so depressed by homesickness that he had absent-mindedly consumed six wedges of it and was being urged to a seventh when some inner voice uttered a saving warning. In spite of very healthy appetites, none of the quartette sought to compete with that record, but Laurie and George did allow themselves to be persuaded to third helpings, declining most politely until they feared to decline any more. Before they had finished, the doctor joined the group and made himself very agreeable, telling several funny stories that set every one laughing and caused a small junior—it was the cherub-faced youth who sat at Laurie's table in the dining-hall and whose career thus far had proved anything but that of a cherub—to swallow a mouthful of mocha cake the wrong way, with disastrous results. During the ensuing confusion the quartette took their departure. At the gate Bob Starling said:

"By the way, fellows, I spoke to Dad about that tennis-court, and he's written to the agent for permission. He says there won't be any trouble; and if there is, he'll agree to put the garden back the way we found it and erect a new arbor."

"What will it be?" asked George. "Sod or gravel?"

"Oh, gravel. You couldn't get a sod court in shape under a year, and I want to use it this fall. I'm going to look around to-morrow for some one to do the job. Know who does that sort of work here—Lee?"

"No, but I suppose you get a contractor; one of those fellows who build roads and stone walls and things."

"I'd ask at the court-house," said Laurie.

"At the court—oh, that's a punk one!" jeered Bob. "See you later, fellows!"

The game with Highland Academy was played across the river at Lookout, and most of the fellows went. In spite of Hop Kendrick's pessimistic prophecy, Hillman's took command of the situation in the first quarter and held it undisturbed to the final whistle. The contest was, if not extremely fast, well played by both teams, and the hosts refused to acknowledge defeat until the end. Captain Stevenson, at left tackle, was the bright, particular star of the day, with the redoubtable Pope a good second.

It was Joe Stevenson's capture of a fumbled ball in the first five minutes of play and his amazing run through the enemy ranks that produced the initial score. Pope kicked an easy goal after Slavin, right half, had plunged through for a touch-down. Later in the game, Pope had added three more points by a place-kick from the forty-two yards. Highland twice reached the Blue's ten-yard line, the first time losing the ball on downs, and the next attempting a forward pass that went astray. Her one opportunity to score by a kick was wrecked by no other than Kewpie, who, having substituted Holmes at the beginning of the second half, somehow shot his hundred and seventy pounds through the defense and met the pigskin with his nose. Kewpie presented a disreputable appearance for several days, but was given due honor. Hillman's returned across the Hudson in the twilight of early October with exultant cheers and songs.

Ned watched that game from the substitutes' bench, just as he had watched the two preceding contests, but a newly awakened *esprit de corps* forbade complaining. When Laurie sympathetically observed that he thought it was time Mulford gave Ned a chance in a real game, Ned responded with dignity, almost with severity, that he guessed the coach knew his business.

The first of the month—or, to be exact, the fourth—brought the twins their monthly allowances, and one of the first things Laurie did was to go to the little blue shop on Pine Street and pay his bill, which had reached its prescribed limit several days before. Ned went, too, although he didn't display much enthusiasm over the mission. Ned held that, having created a bill, it was all wrong deliberately to destroy it. To his mind, a bill was something to cherish and preserve. Laurie, however, pointed out that, since one was prohibited from further transactions at the Widow's, even on a cash basis, as long as one owed money there, it would be wise to cancel the debts. Ned recognized the wisdom of the statement and reluctantly parted with ninety-seven cents.

Since it was only a little after two o'clock, the shop was empty when the twins entered, and Polly and her mother were just finishing their lunch in the back room. It was Polly who answered the tinkle of the bell and who, after some frowning and turning of pages in the account-book, canceled the indebtedness.

"Now," said Ned, "I guess I'll have a cream-cake. Want one, Laurie?"

Laurie did, in spite of the fact that it was less than an hour since dinner. Mrs. Deane appeared at the door, observed the proceeding, and smiled.

"I'm real glad to see you're still alive," she said to Ned. "I guess he must take very good care of you."

"Yes'm, I do," Laurie assured her gravely.

Ned laughed scornfully, or as scornfully as it was possible to laugh with his mouth full. "You shouldn't believe everything he tells you, Mrs. Deane. I have to look after him like a baby. Why, he wouldn't get down in time for breakfast if I didn't put most of his clothes on."

"That's no joke, either," retorted Laurie, "about you putting my clothes on. You're wearing one of my collars and my best socks right now, and—yes, sir, that's my blue tie!"

"Wait a bit, partner! Where'd you get that shirt you're wearing?"

"That's different," answered Laurie, with dignity. "Mine are all in the wash. Besides, it's an old one and you never wear it."

"I never get a chance to wear it!"

"It must be very convenient for you," said Mrs. Deane, smilingly, "to be able to wear each other's things. Polly, I guess there won't be any one else in for a while; maybe they'd like to see your garden."

Being assured that they would, Polly led the way through the back room, a pleasant, sunny apartment evidently combining the duties of kitchen and dining-room, and out to a little back porch shaded by morning-glories and nasturtiums that fairly ran riot over the green lattice. There was a braided rug on the floor and a small rocker and a tiny table on which were books and a magazine or two. The books were evidently Polly's school books, for they were held together by a strap.

The twins liked that garden. It wasn't very large, for when the peculiar Mr. Coventry had divided the estate he had placed the high board fence very close to the little frame dwelling; but perhaps its very smallness made it seem more attractive. Narrow beds encompassed it on three sides, and a gravel walk followed the beds. In the tiny square inside, a small rustic arbor, covered with climbing rose-vines, held a seat that, as was presently proved, accommodated three very comfortably.

But before they were allowed to sit down the boys had to be shown many things: the hollyhocks against the back fence, the flowering almond that had been brought all the way from the old home in New Jersey,—and had never quite made up its mind whether to die of homesickness or go on living,— the bed of lilies-of-the-valley that just *wouldn't* keep out of the path and many other floral treasures. Nasturtiums and morning-glories and scarlet sage and crinkly-edged white and lavender petunias were still blossoming gaily, and there was even a cluster of white roses on the arbor, for, so far, no frost had come. The twins admired properly and Polly was all smiles, until suddenly she said, "O-oh!" and faced them reproachfully.

"You've just let me go on and be perfectly ridiculous!" she charged. "I don't think it's a bit nice of you!"

"Why, what—how do you mean?" stammered Ned.

"You have the most wonderful flowers in the world in California, and you know it!" she replied severely; "and you've let me show you these poor little things as if—as if they were anything at all in comparison! I forgot you came from California."

"Maybe we didn't tell you," offered Laurie. "Anyway, your flowers—"

"In California they have hedges of geraniums and roses climb right over the houses, and orange-trees and palms and everything," interrupted Polly, breathlessly. "Why, this garden must seem perfectly—perfectly *awful* to you!"

"Don't you believe it!" denied Ned. "Flowers and things do grow bigger, I suppose, out our way; but they aren't a bit prettier, are they, Laurie?"

"Not so pretty," answered the other, earnestly. "Besides, *I* never saw a geranium hedge in my life. Maybe they have them in some places, like Pasadena, but there isn't *one* in Santa Lucia, honest. There isn't, is there, Ned?"

"*I* never saw one. And palms aren't awfully pretty. They get sort of scraggly-looking sometimes. Honest, Polly, I never saw a garden any prettier and cuter than this is. Of course, some are bigger and—and more magnificent—"

"Who wants a magnificent garden?" demanded Laurie, scornfully. "What have you got in the box, Polly?"

Comforted, Polly smiled again. "That's Antoinette," she said. "Come and see."

Antoinette lived in a wooden box in the shelter of the porch, and had long ears and very blue eyes and a nose that twitched funnily when they approached. In short, Antoinette was a fluffy smoke-gray rabbit. "She has a dreadfully long pedigree," said Polly, as she took Antoinette out and snuggled her in her arms.

"Has she?" murmured Laurie. "I thought it looked rather short."

"A pedigree isn't a *tail*, you idiot," said Ned, scathingly. "She's awfully pretty, Polly. Will she bite?"

"Of course not! At least, not unless you look like a cabbage-leaf."

"I wouldn't take a chance," Laurie advised. "Any one who's as green as you are—"

"She *tries* to eat 'most everything," said Polly, "but she likes cabbage and lettuce and carrots best."

"I wish I had a cabbage," muttered Laurie, searching his pockets; "or a carrot. You haven't a carrot with you, have you, Ned?"

"You're the silliest boys!" laughed Polly, returning Antoinette to her box. "Let's go and sit down a minute." And when they were on the seat under the arbor and she had smoothed her skirt and tucked a pair of rather soiled white canvas shoes from sight, she announced, "There! Now you can make up a verse about something!"

CHAPTER X
POLLY ENTERTAINS

"Make up a—what did you say?" asked Ned.

"Make up a verse," answered Polly, placidly. "As you did the other day when you went out. Don't you remember?"

"Oh!" Laurie looked somewhat embarrassed and a trifle silly. "Why, you see—we only do that when—when—"

"When we have inspiration," aided Ned, glibly.

"Yes, that's it, inspiration! We—we have to have inspiration."

"I'm sure Antoinette ought to be enough inspiration to any poet," returned Polly, laughing. "You know you never saw a more beautiful rabbit in your life—lives, I mean."

Ned looked inquiringly at Laurie. Then he said, "Well, maybe if I close my eyes a minute—" He suited action to word. Polly viewed him with eager interest; Laurie, with misgiving. Finally, after a moment of silent suspense, his eyelids flickered and:

"O Antoinette, most lovely of thy kind!" he declaimed.

"Thou eatest cabbages and watermelon rind!" finished Laurie, promptly.

Polly clapped her hands, but her approval was short-lived. "But she doesn't eatest watermelon rind," she declared indignantly. "I'm sure it wouldn't be at all good for her!"

Laurie grinned. "That's what we call poetic license," he explained. "When you make a rhyme, sometimes you've got to—to sacrifice truth for—in the interests of—I mean, you've got to think of the *sound*! 'Kind' and 'carrot' wouldn't sound *right*, don't you see?"

"Well, I'm sure watermelon rind doesn't sound right, either," objected Polly; "not for a rabbit. Rabbits have very delicate digestions."

"We might change it," offered Ned. "How would this do?

"O Antoinette, more lovely than a parrot,
Thou dost subsist on cabbages and carrot."

"That's silly," said Polly, scornfully.

"Poetry usually is silly," Ned answered.

Laurie, who had been gazing raptly at his shoes, broke forth exultantly. "I've got it!" he cried. "Listen!

"O Antoinette, most beauteous of rabbits,
Be mine and I will feed thee naught but cabbits!"

A brief silence followed. Then Ned asked, "What are cabbits?"

"Cabbits are vegetables," replied Laurie.

"I never heard of them," said Polly, wrinkling her forehead.

"Neither did any one else," laughed Ned. "He just made them up to rhyme with rabbits."

"A cabbit," said Laurie, loftily, "is something between a cabbage and a carrot."

"What does it look like?" giggled Polly.

Laurie blinked. "We-ell, you've seen a—you've seen an artichoke, haven't you?" Polly nodded and Laurie blinked again. "And you've seen a—a mangel-wurzel?"

"No, I don't think so."

"Then I don't see how I can tell you," said Laurie, evidently relieved, "because a cabbit is more like a mangel-wurzel than anything else. Of course, it's not so deciduous, and the shape is different; it's more obvate than a mangel-wurzel; more—" he swept his hands vaguely in air—"more phenomenal."

"Oh, dry up," said Ned, grinning. "How'd you like to have to put up with an idiot like that all your life, Polly? The worst of it is, folks sometimes mistake him for me!"

"Yes, it's awful, but I manage to bear up under it," Laurie sighed.

"How did you ever come to think of making those funny rhymes?" Polly asked.

"Oh, we had measles once, about four years ago," said Ned. "We always had everything together—measles, whooping-cough, scarlet fever, everything. And when we were getting over it they wouldn't let us read and so we made up rhymes. I forget whose idea it was. I'd make up one line and Laurie would make up the other, or the other way round. The idea was to have the last word of the first line so hard that the other fellow couldn't rhyme to it. But I guess I only stuck Laurie once. Then the word was lemon."

"You didn't really stick me then," Laurie denied. "I rhymed it with demon. You said they didn't rhyme, but I showed you a rhyming dictionary that said they did."

"The dictionary said it was an imperfect rhyme, Laurie, and—"

"Just the same, a rhyme's a rhyme. Say, Ned, remember the one we made up about Miss Yetter?" Ned nodded and grinned. "Miss Yetter was our nurse. We thought it was pretty clever, but she didn't like it.

"When feeling ill send for Miss Yetter.
If you don't die, she'll make you better."

"She was quite insulted about it," laughed Ned, "and told Dad; and he tried to lecture us, but we got laughing so he couldn't. We made rhymes all the time for a while and nearly drove folks crazy; and finally Dad said if we didn't stop it he'd whale us. And I said, 'All right, sir, we'll try not to do it'; and Laurie, the chump, butted in with, "Cause if we do, we know we'll rue it!' We nearly got the licking right then!"

"You *are* funny!" laughed Polly. "Is your mother—haven't you—"

"She died when we were kids," answered Laurie. "I just remember her, but Ned doesn't."

"You think you do. You've just heard Dad, and nurse talk about her. We were only four when Mother died."

Laurie looked unconvinced, but didn't argue the matter. Instead he asked, "Your father's dead, isn't he, Polly?"

"Yes, he died when I was eight. He was a dear, and I missed him just terribly. Mother says I look like him. He was very tall and was always laughing. Mother says he laughed so much he didn't have time for anything else. She means that he wasn't—wasn't very successful. We were very poor when he died. But I guess he was lots nicer than he would have been if he had just been—successful. I guess the most successful man in this town is Mr. Sparks, the banker, and no one has ever seen him laugh once. And Uncle Peter was successful, too, I suppose; and he was just as sour and ill-tempered as anything. He wasn't my real uncle, but I called him that because Mother said it would please him. It didn't seem to."

"Was that Mr. Coventry?" asked Laurie. "The mis—I mean the man who lived in the big square house over there?"

"Yes. And I don't mind your calling him the miser, because that is just what he was. He was Mother's half-brother, but he didn't act as if he was even a quarter-brother! He was always just as horrid as he could be. When Father died he wrote Mother to come here and he would provide her with a home. And when we came, we found he meant that Mother was to live here and pay him rent. She didn't have enough money to do that, and so Uncle Peter made the front of the house into a store and bought some things for her and made her sign a mortgage or something. When he died, we thought maybe he had left Mother a little; but there wasn't any will, and not much property, either—just the big house on Walnut Street and this place and about two thousand dollars. When the property was divided, Mother got the other heirs to let her have this as her portion of the estate, but she had to pay four hundred and fifty dollars for it. That took about all she had saved and more, and so we haven't been able to do much to the house yet."

"It doesn't look as if it needed much doing to," said Ned, critically.

"Oh, but it does! It needs a new coat of paint, for one thing. And some of the blinds are broken. And there ought to be a furnace in it. Stoves don't really keep it warm in winter. Some day we'll fix it up nicely, though. As soon as I get through high school, I'm going to work and make a lot of money."

"Attaboy!" approved Ned. "What are you going to do, Polly?"

"I'm learning stenography and typewriting, and Mr. Farmer, the lawyer,—he's the one who got the others to let Mother have the house when Uncle Peter's estate was settled,—says he will find a place for me in his office. He's awfully nice. Some stenographers make lots of money, don't they?"

"I guess so," Ned agreed. "There's a woman in Dad's office who gets eighteen dollars a week."

Polly clasped her hands delightedly. "Maybe I wouldn't get that much, though. I guess Mr. Farmer doesn't pay his stenographer very high wages. Maybe I'd get twelve dollars, though. Don't you think I might?"

"Sure!" said Laurie. "Don't you let any one tell you any different. Didn't folks think that your Uncle Peter left more money than was found, Polly?"

"Oh, yes; but no one really knew. The lawyers looked everywhere. If he did have any more, he must have hidden it away pretty well. They looked all through the house and dug holes in the cellar floor. It was very exciting. Mother thinks he lost what money he had speculating in stocks and things. He used to go to New York about four times a year. No one knew what he did there, not even Hilary; but Mother thinks he went to see men who deal in stocks and that they got his money away from him."

"Who is Hilary?" Laurie inquired.

"Hilary was a colored man that Uncle had had a long time. It seemed to me that if Uncle had had much money, Hilary would have known about it; and he didn't."

"Where is he now? Hilary, I mean," added Laurie, somewhat unnecessarily.

"I don't know. He went away a little while after Uncle Peter died. He said he was going to New York, I think."

"You don't suppose he took the money with him, do you? I mean—"

"Oh no!" Polly seemed quite horrified. "Hilary was just as honest as honest! Why, Uncle Peter died owing him almost forty dollars and Hilary never got a cent of it! The lawyers were too mean for anything!"

"There's a fellow named Starling living there now," Laurie said. "His father's rented the house for three years. Bob says that he's going to find the money and give it to your mother."

Polly laughed. "Oh, I wish that he would! But I guess if the lawyers couldn't find it he never will. Lawyers, they say, can find money when nobody else can! Is he nice?"

"Bob? Yes, he's a dandy chap. You ought to know him, Polly; he's your next-door neighbor."

"Back-door neighbor, you mean," interpolated Ned.

"I think I saw him in the garden one day," said Polly. "His father is an engineer, Mae Ferrand says, and he's building a big bridge for the railway. Or maybe it's a tunnel. I forget."

"Is Mae Something the girl with the molasses-candy hair you were with at the high school game?" Laurie asked.

"Yes, but her hair isn't like molasses candy. It's perfectly lovely hair. It's like—like diluted sunshine!"

Laurie whistled. "Gee! Did you get that, Neddie? Well, anyway, I like dark hair better."

"Oh, I don't! I'd love to have hair like Mae's. And, what do you think, she likes my hair better than her own!"

"Don't blame her," said Laurie. "What do you say, Ned?"

"I say I've got to beat it back and get into football togs. What time is it?"

"Look at your own watch, you lazy loafer. Well, come on. I say, Polly, would your mother let you go to the game with me Saturday? That is, if you want to, of course."

"Oh, I'd love to! But—I'll ask her, anyway. And if she says I may, would you mind if Mae went too? We usually go together to the games."

"Not a bit. I'll be around again before Saturday and see what she says."

"I wouldn't be surprised if she said yes," remarked Polly. "I think she must like you boys. Anyway, you're the first of the Hillman's boys she has ever let me invite out here."

"Really? Bully for her! Wait till I say farewell to Antoinette, 'most beauteous of rabbits!' What does she twitch her nose like that for?"

"I think she's asking for some cabbits," replied Polly, gravely.

"She's making faces at you, you chump," said Ned, rudely. "Come on." They returned through the little living-room, empty save for a big black cat asleep in a rocking-chair, and found Mrs. Deane serving the first of the afternoon trade in the shop beyond. They said good afternoon to her very politely, and Polly went to the door with them. Outside on the walk, Ned nudged Laurie, and they paused side by side and gravely removed their caps.

"We give you thanks and say farewell, Miss Polly."

"The visit's been, indeed, most jolly!"

CHAPTER XI
NED SPEAKS OUT

There was a cut in the football squad that afternoon and more than a dozen candidates were retired, leaving twenty-eight players for the first and scrub teams. Ned survived, as, indeed, he expected to; for, while he knew his limitations, neither the coach nor the captain appeared to. Perhaps they were sometimes puzzled over flashes of ineptitude, or perhaps they put them down to temporary reversals of form; at least, Ned's talent was never seriously questioned by them. He had settled down as a regular half-back on the scrub eleven, although twice he had been called on in practice scrimmages to take Mason's place at left half on the first squad. He was too light to make much headway in bucking plays, and his inability to start quickly handicapped him frequently in running; but as a kicker he was dependable and had developed a quite remarkable accuracy at forward passing. Against a light opponent or a slow one he could be counted on to play a fairly good game, although so far he had not been allowed the opportunity. With him on the scrub team was Hop Kendrick at quarter, and, for a time, Kewpie at center. But Kewpie had trained down at last to a hundred and sixty-five pounds and was handling his weight and bulk with a new snappiness, and a few days after Ned became a part of the scrub outfit Kewpie was elevated to the first team, and a much disgruntled Holmes took his place on the second.

With the defeat of Wagner School, Hillman's ended her preliminary season. In that contest, played at home, the Blue showed a new aggressiveness and much more speed; and, while she was able to score only one touch-down, and Pope failed miserably at goal, every one was well satisfied. Wagner had a strong team, and a victory over it was no small triumph. Hillman's line held splendidly under the battering-ram tactics of the adversary, and her backs were fast and shifty. On attack, the Blue failed to gain consistently; but in the third period, with a captured fumble on Wagner's thirty-three yards for encouragement, Pope got free for half the distance, and Slavin and Mason, alternating, worked the enemy's left side until the ball lay on the five-yard line. Then a fake attack on Wagner's right, with Pope carrying the ball through on the left of center, brought the only score of the day. Kewpie proved himself that afternoon, for he was a veritable Rock of Gibraltar on defense and a hundred and sixty-five pounds of steel springs on attack. The Blue team was far from a perfect machine yet, but it seemed that Mulford had found his parts and that only a generous oiling was needed.

Laurie and George Watson escorted Polly and Mae Ferrand to the game, and, although aware of the covert grins and whispered witticisms of acquaintances, enjoyed themselves hugely. Mae proved to be a very jolly, wholesome sort of girl, and her knowledge of what may be termed "inside football" was stupendous and made both Laurie and George rather ashamed of their ignorance. Between the halves, Ned, arrayed in a trailing gray blanket, joined them and promptly became involved with Mae in a very technical argument that no one else could follow. From the fact that Ned retired with a rather dispirited expression when the teams came on again, Laurie surmised that the honors had gone to Mae.

The following Monday evening, while the enthusiasm produced by the victory over Wagner School was still undiminished, a second mass-meeting was held in the auditorium to devise means of replenishing the football treasury: Three of the remaining five games were to be played away from Orstead, and in two cases the distance to be traveled was considerable and the expenses consequently large. As Joe Stevenson said, introducing the subject for discussion, if Hillman's charged admission to her home games, it would be possible to get through a season without asking for assistance from the student body. "But you fellows know that that isn't the school policy. We are allowed to sell tickets for the Farview game only, and, while we make about four hundred and fifty dollars as our share, that doesn't go very far against the season's outlay. We have to pay from seventy-five to a hundred and twenty-five dollars to every team that comes here to play us. When we go away we seldom make enough to pay our expenses. In the Highland game, because it cost us almost nothing for fares, we did. At the present moment we have a cash balance on hand of forty-three dollars, and our liabilities, including Mr. Mulford's salary for the remainder of the season, are about eight hundred dollars.

"The manager estimates that we'll have to incur added expenses for about a hundred and twenty dollars for Farview game tickets and new supplies. In short, we shall have to pay out, before the season ends, about nine hundred dollars. Against that we have on hand forty-three dollars, and in prospect something like five hundred, leaving us about three hundred and fifty in the hole.

"There has been talk of cutting out the Lansing and Whittier games, but that wouldn't make enough difference. Besides, it would give us a black eye to cancel games as late as this. We might save perhaps seventy dollars if we did, but it would cost us ten times that in public estimation. As far as I can see, fellows, if we're going to have a football team, we've got to pay for it. We've asked permission to charge admission, even a nominal one, to all games, but the faculty is against it. And we have asked to have a regular assessment made against each student. To many of us that would seem the fairer and most satisfactory way of meeting the emergency. But the faculty doesn't like that any better than the other proposition. So I guess it's up to us, each and every one of us, to dig down and produce the coin.

"We need three hundred and fifty dollars at least. That means that every fellow in school must pony up four dollars, or, rather, that the average must be four dollars each. Some of you can't give so much, probably, and a few can give more. I'd like to hear from you, please. Don't be afraid to say what you think. We want to get together on this matter and thrash it out, if it takes until ten o'clock. Any one who has any suggestion to offer or anything to say will be heard. Come on, somebody!"

There were plenty of speakers: Dave Brewster, the baseball captain, Dan Whipple, senior class president, Lew Cooper, upper middle class president, Dave Murray, the manager of the team, Craig Jones, for the lower middlers, and many others, Some subscribed to the donation scheme, others opposed it. Cooper suggested an appeal to the school alumni. Brewster pointed out that the effort would cost money and that the result would be uncertain and, in any case, slow. An increase in the price of tickets to the Farview game was discussed and the idea abandoned. An hour passed and the meeting was getting nowhere. Some of the younger boys had already withdrawn. A tall, lantern-jawed youth had charged the football committee with extravagance, and Dave Murray had bitterly resented the allegation. Ned, who, with Laurie and Lee Murdock, was seated near the back of the hall, had shown signs of restiveness for some time and had been muttering to himself. Now, to the surprise of his companions, he jumped to his feet and demanded recognition:

"Mr. Chairman!"

"Mister—" Dan Whipple pointed a finger at Ned and nodded.

"Turner," prompted Kewpie from a front seat.

"Mr. Turner," encouraged the chairman.

"I'd like to say that I never heard so much talking and saw so little action," began Ned, impatiently. "What's the matter with some one saying something useful instead of just chewing the rag?"

"You tell 'em," piped a small junior, above the applause and laughter.

"All right! I'll tell you fellows that you're a lot of pikers to hesitate to pledge three or four hundred dollars to keep your team going. Where I come from we had to have a new grand stand two years ago, and we called a meeting like this and we raised seven hundred dollars in thirty-five minutes in cash and pledges. There were a lot more of us, but half of us would have felt like Rockefellers if we'd ever found a whole half-dollar in our pockets! Some of us gave as high as five dollars, but not many. Most of us pledged two dollars; and those who didn't have two dollars went out and worked until they'd made it, by jingo! And we got our grand stand up inside of two weeks, in time for the big baseball game."

There was real applause this time, and those in the front of the hall had swung around to have a look at the earnest youth who was calling them names.

"That's one way of getting the money," continued Ned, warming up finely, "but there's another. Out my way—"

"Say, where do you come from?" called some one.

"I come from California," answered Ned, proudly. "Maybe you've heard of it!"

"Attaboy!" shouted Kewpie. "Swing your leg, Nid!"

"When we want to raise some money out there and folks are too stingy to give it outright, we take it away from them another way. We get up a fête. We give them a good time and they pay for it. Why not try it here? I don't know how many folks there are in this burg, but I reckon there are enough to part with three or four hundred dollars. Give them an excuse to spend their money and they'll spend it!"

Ned sat down amid loud applause, and Dave Brewster was recognized, although half a dozen others were clamoring for speech.

"Turner's said something, fellows," declared Brewster. "The idea's worth considering. We've never tackled the town folks for money, and there's no reason why they shouldn't come across. They've come to our games for years without paying a cent, except for the Farview game, and it wouldn't hurt them to give a little to a good cause. I don't know what sort of a fête Turner has in mind, but I should think we might get up something that would do the business."

"Mr. Chairman," said Kewpie, "I move that a committee of three be appointed by the chair, to include Nid,—I mean Mr. Turner,—to consider the—the matter of giving a fête to raise the money."

"Seconded!"

"You have heard the motion," droned Whipple. "All those in favor will so signify by saying 'Aye.' Contrary, 'No.' Moved and carried. I will appoint the presidents of the senior and upper middle classes and Mr. Turner to the committee, three in all. Is it the sense of this meeting that your committee is to report to it at a subsequent meeting, or is it to have authority to proceed with the matter if it decides that the scheme is a good one?"

"Full authority, Mr. Chairman!" "Let 'em go ahead with it!" "Sure! That's what we want. Let's have action!"

"Is there any other business? Then I declare the meeting adjourned!"

Whipple captured Ned on the way out. "We'd better get together right away on this, Turner," he said. "Can you meet Cooper and me at my room to-morrow at twelve?"

Ned agreed, and he and Laurie and Lee went on. "What I'd like to know," remarked Laurie, after a moment's silence, "is how you're going to have a fête in a place like this. The weather's too cold for it."

"Maybe it will be warmer," answered Ned, cheerfully. "Besides, we don't have to have it outdoors."

"It wouldn't be a fête if you didn't," sniffed the other.

"Well, what's the difference? Call it anything you like. The big thing is to get the money."

"You had your cheek with you to talk the way you did," chuckled Laurie.

"He talked sense, though," asserted Lee, warmly.

"Of course. The Turners always do." Laurie steered Ned toward the entrance of East Hall. "Well, good night, Lee. See you at the fête!"

Upstairs, Ned tossed his cap to the bed, plumped himself into a chair at the table, and drew paper and pencil to him. "Now," he said, "let's figure this out. I've got to talk turkey to those fellows to-morrow. What's your idea, partner?"

"Hey, where do you get that stuff?" demanded Laurie. "Why drag me into it? It's not my fête. I don't own it."

"Shut up and sit down there before I punch your head. You've got to help with this. The honor of the Turners is at stake!"

So Laurie subsided and for more than an hour he and Ned racked their brains and gradually the plan took shape.

CHAPTER XII
THE COMMITTEE ON ARRANGEMENTS

"It's like this," explained Ned. He and Laurie and Polly and Mae Ferrand were in the little garden behind the shop. The girls were on the bench and the boys were seated on the turf before the arbor, their knees encircled with their arms. A few yards away Antoinette eyed them gravely and twitched her nose. On the porch step, Towser, the big black cat, blinked benignly, sometimes shifting his gaze to the branches of the maple in the next yard, where an impudent black-and-white woodpecker was seeking a late luncheon.

"There are two sub-committees," continued Ned, earnestly. "Whipple and Cooper are the Committee on Finance and Publicity, and Laurie and I are the Committee on Arrangements. I told them I had to have help and so they took Laurie in."

"No thanks to you," grumbled Laurie, who was, however, secretly much pleased.

"It's going to be next Saturday afternoon and evening, and this is Tuesday, and so there isn't much time. We were afraid to make it any later because the weather might get too cold. Besides, the team needs the money right off. I looked in an almanac and it said that next Saturday would be fair and warm, so that's all right."

"But don't you think almanacs make mistakes sometimes?" asked Polly. "I know ours does. When we had our high-school picnic, the almanac said 'showers' and it was a perfectly gorgeous day. I carried my mackintosh around all day and it was a perfect nuisance. Don't you remember, Mae?"

"Well, you've got to believe in something," declared Ned. "Anyway, we're going to have it at Bob Starling's, and if it's too cold outdoors, we'll move inside."

"You mean at Uncle Peter's?" exclaimed Polly.

"Yes. We thought of having it at school first, but Mr. Hillman didn't like it much; and besides, the fellows would be inside without having to pay to get there! You see, it's going to cost every one a quarter just to get in."

"And how much to get out?" asked Mae, innocently.

Ned grinned. "As much as we can get away from them. There'll be twelve booths to sell things in—"

"What sort of things?" Polly inquired.

"All sorts. Eats and drinks and everything. We're getting the storekeepers to donate things. So far they've just given us things that they haven't been able to sell, a pile of junk; but we're going to stop that. Biddle, the hardware man, gave us a dozen cheap pocket-knives, but he's got to come across again. We've been to only eight of them so far, but we haven't done so worse. Guess we've got enough truck for one booth already. And then there'll be one of them for a rummage sale. We're going to get each of the fellows to give us something for that, and I'll bet we'll have a fine lot of truck. Each booth will represent a college and be decorated in the proper colors: Yale, Harvard, Princeton, and so on. And—and now it's your turn, Laurie."

"Yes, I notice that I always have to do the dirty work," said the other. He hugged his knees tighter, rolled over on his back for inspiration, and, when he again faced his audience on the bench, smiled his nicest. "Here's where you girls come in," he announced. "We want you two to take two of the booths and get a girl for each of the others. Want to?"

"Oh, it would be darling!" cried Polly.

"I'd love to!" said Mae.

"Only—"

"Only—"

"Only what!" asked Ned, as the girls viewed each other doubtfully.

"I'm not sure Mother would let me," sighed Polly. "Do you think she would, Mae?"

"I don't believe so. And I don't believe Mama would let me. She—she's awfully particular that way."

"Gee!" said Ned, in disappointed tones, "I don't see why not! It isn't as if—"

"Of course it isn't," agreed Laurie. "Besides, your mothers would be there too!"

"Would they?" asked Mae, uncertainly.

"Of course! Every one's coming! What harm would there be in it? You can do things for—for charity that you can't do any other time! All you'd have to do would be to just stand behind the booth and sell things. It won't be hard. Everything will have the price marked on it and—"

"You won't need to go by the prices always, though," interpolated Ned. "I mean, if you can get more than the thing is marked, you'd better do it! And then there's the—the costumes, Laurie."

"Oh, yes, I forgot. We'd like each girl to sort of wear something that would sort of match the college she represented—sort of," he explained apologetically. "If you had the Yale booth, you could wear a dark-blue waist, and so on. Do you think that would be possible?"

Polly giggled. "We might ask Stella Hatch to take the Harvard booth, Mae. With her hair, she wouldn't have to dress much!"

"And you and Polly could take your first pick," observed Laurie, craftily. "You'd look swell as—as Dartmouth, Mae!"

"In *green*! My gracious, Ned! No, thank you! But Polly ought to be Yale. She looks lovely in blue. I think I'd like to be Cornell. My brother Harry's in Cornell."

"All right," agreed Ned. "I wish you'd ask your mothers soon, will you? Do try, because we've just got to get girls for the booths. You'd have lots of fun, too. The Banjo and Mandolin Club is going to play for dancing for an hour at five and nine, and there'll be an entertainment, too."

"What sort?" asked Polly.

"We don't know yet. Some of the gymnastic team will do stunts, I think, for one thing, and there'll be singing and maybe Laurie will do some rope-swinging—"

"I told you a dozen times I wouldn't! Besides, I haven't any rope."

"We can find one, probably," replied his brother, untroubled. "We haven't settled about the entertainment yet. And there are two or three other things we haven't got to. Starling's going to have his garden all fixed up, and he's going to cover the old arbor with branches and hang Chinese lanterns in it and have little tables and chairs there for folks to sit down and eat ice-cream and cake.

"And that reminds me, Polly. Do you suppose that Miss Comfort would make some cakes for us?"

"Why, yes, Nid, but—but you'd have to *buy* them. I don't think you ought to expect her to *donate* them."

"We meant to buy them, of course, Polly. And we wondered if your mother would make some of those dandy cream-puffs."

"I'm sure she will. How many would you want?"

"I don't know. You see, there's no way of telling how many will come. There are three thousand people in Orstead, but that doesn't mean much, does it? The 'Messenger' editor's agreed to put in an advertisement for us for nothing, and there'll be notices all around town in the windows: we got the man who prints the school monthly to do them for just the cost of the paper. So folks ought to come, shouldn't you think?"

"Oh, I'm sure they will!" agreed Polly, and Mae echoed her. "But it'll be dreadfully hard to know how much cake and ice-cream and refreshments to order, won't it?"

"Fierce," agreed Ned. "I suppose the best way will be to reckon on, say, three hundred and order that much stuff. Only, how do you tell how much three hundred will eat?"

"Why, you can't! Besides, Nid, three hundred people would only bring in seventy-five dollars!"

"In admissions, yes; but we've got to make them buy things when we get them in there. If every one spent a dollar inside—"

"But lots of them won't. Do you think they will, Mae?"

Mae shook her head. "No, I don't. Lots and lots will just come out of curiosity and won't spend a cent. I know, boys, because that's the way they act at the fairs here."

Ned kicked at the turf gloomily. "Gee, that's fierce!" he muttered.

"Well, we'd ought to get more than three hundred folks," said Laurie. "Remember, it's to be afternoon and evening too. I'll bet there'll be nearer six hundred than three."

Ned brightened. "That's so. And six hundred, even if they only averaged fifty cents apiece, would be three hundred dollars. And I guess if we can make three hundred, we can dig up the other fifty! Well, we've got to get busy, Laurie. I got them to give me a cut from practice this afternoon and I'll have to make the most of my time," he explained to the girls.

"Oh! And did they let you off, too, Nod?" asked Polly.

"No, we're through with baseball," Laurie answered. "No more till spring. I'm just fairly broken-hearted!"

"When will you know about helping us, Polly?" Ned asked.

"But don't you think almanacs make mistakes sometimes?" asked Polly

"I'll ask Mother right away; and you'll ask, too, won't you, Mae? Can you stop in this evening? I do hope it'll be all right!"

"So do we!" said Ned and Laurie, in a breath. "Rather!"

And the Committee on Arrangements hurried away.

That night the committee met again in Dan Whipple's room in West Hall and satisfactory progress was reported all along the line. Ned read a list of donations from the town merchants, and announced that twelve young ladies from the high school would be on hand, appropriately attired, to take charge of the booths. Lew Cooper showed proofs of the poster that was to be displayed in windows and tacked on posts and fences, and of the four-inch, double-column advertisement to appear in the "Messenger." Dan reported that Mr. Wells, the physical director, had promised to see that the best six members of the gymnastic team should exhibit afternoon and evening.

"That means, though," he said, "that we'll have to have some kind of a platform. Better make a note of that, Lew."

"Platforms cost money," answered Lew, dubiously. "Maybe we can borrow—I'll tell you what! There's one stored over in the field-house, one they use to set the dressing-tent on. It's in two pieces,—sections,—but I guess it's big enough. We'll see if we can't get the use of it."

"Good! Better ask Mr. Wells, Say, Hal, did you see Norris?"

Hal Pringle was Dan's room-mate, and, while he was usually present at the meetings, he was careful to keep himself in the background unless called on for advice. Now he looked up from his book and nodded. "Yes, it 'a all right. They'll play for an hour in the afternoon and an hour at night. I had to promise them eats, though."

"Of course. Much obliged. Speaking of eats, fellows, what's been done about the refreshments?"

"Nothing yet," answered Ned. "I wanted to talk that over. How many sandwiches and how much salad will we want? And how many gallons of ice-cream and—"

"Whoa!" begged Dan. "Blessed if I know! How the dickens are we going to know how much food will be needed? What's the rule about it? Or isn't there any?"

"Depends on how many will attend the show," said Lew. "Find that out—"

"How're we going to find it out, you chump? How many do you suppose we can count on, Ned?"

"Maybe six hundred," was the answer. "But if it should rain—"

"There you are! If it rained, we mightn't get two hundred! I'll say that's a problem. We'd be in a fine fix if we found ourselves with two or three freezers of ice-cream on our hands and a lot of other truck. Look here, Tabby might know. Suppose you ask her, Ned. We've got to have enough and not too much."

"It'll be all right about the ice-cream," said Laurie. "The man said we could return what we didn't open if we got it back that night so he could pack it over. But the other things—"

"You talk to Tabby in the morning," repeated Dan. "She'll know if any one does. Now what else? What about the entertainment part of it, Mr. Chairman of the Committee on Arrangements? What have you got in mind besides the gymnastics?"

"We thought we might find some one who could sing or dance. But we don't know many of the fellows."

"Bully! There's Cheesman, Lew. He's a corker. And Kewpie isn't so bad. He sings a funny song mighty well."

"He couldn't sing it in the afternoon, though, Dan: he'd be at the field."

"That's so! still, the game ought to be finished by four. We wouldn't have the entertainment part until late, would we?"

"About four, I thought," said Ned, "but Kewpie could come last. I'll put him down, anyway."

"Anything else besides songs?" asked Dan.

"Yes, only-" Ned dropped his voice and glanced at Pringle—"only it's got to be kept a secret to make good."

"Oh, Hal's all right. He's a sort of ex-officio member of the committee. Shoot, Ned!"

CHAPTER XIII
NED GETS INTO THE GAME

Four hectic days followed. To Laurie, since Ned was held for two hours each afternoon at the football field, fell most of the duties of the Committee on Arrangements, and he was a very busy youth. He badgered shopkeepers into parting with goods to be sold at the booths, helped Bob Starling trim up the old arbor in the garden of the Coventry place, made frequent trips to the Or stead caterer's, engaged eight cakes from Miss Comfort and twelve dozen cream-puffs from the Widow Deane, spent two hours Wednesday helping Lew and Hal Pringle distribute posters throughout the village, and attended to a hundred other matters between-times. Of course, Ned aided when he could, and was helpful with advice and unfailing in suggestions; but recitations and football practice didn't leave him much time, even though he conscientiously arose a full hour earlier every morning that week, and skimped studying so much that he got in trouble with three instructors in one day!

Miss Tabitha had proved as helpful as Dan Whipple had predicted. She had shaken her head at the idea of entertaining six hundred at the fête. "You mustn't count on more than half that many," she said. "I dare say all the boys will go, and they'll make ninety. Then, if you get two hundred of the townsfolk, you'll be doing very nicely. Don't decide how much salad or how many sandwiches you want until Saturday morning. So much will depend on the weather. Even if you hold the affair indoors, lots of folks won't come if it rains. You say you've ordered eight cakes from Martha Comfort and twelve dozen cream-puffs from Mrs. Deane?"

"Yes'm," said Ned. "We wanted Mrs. Deane to make more, but she didn't think she could."

"Well, that's a hundred and fourty-four cream-puffs, and—let me see—one of Miss Comfort's cakes will cut into sixteen pieces, and eight times sixteen—"

"A hundred and twenty-eight, ma'am."

"Well, and a hundred and twenty-eight and a hundred and forty-four—"

"Two hundred and seventy-two."

"You're real quick at figures, aren't you? Seems as if, though, counting on three hundred, you'd be a little short. I'll have Aunt Persis make one of her marble-cakes. That'll help out, I guess."

"Yes'm; thanks awfully," answered Ned.

"Who is going to serve the refreshments?"

"Why—why—" Ned's face fell. "I guess we hadn't thought of that!"

"Well, it makes a heap of difference, because you can make a quart of ice-cream serve ten people or twenty, just as you've a mind to. I usually count on sixteen. Same way with a loaf of cake, and same way with salad. It's awfully easy to waste salad when you're serving it. Now, if you'd like me to, Ned, I'll attend to serving everything for you. You just have the things set down there and I'll look after them."

"Oh, Miss Hillman, if you would! Gee, that would be great! It—it'll be a lot of trouble, though, ma'am."

"Well, I guess it won't be the first trouble I've seen," replied Miss Tabitha, dryly; "nor it won't be the last!"

Thursday afternoon Laurie hurried over to the Coventry place as soon as a two-o'clock recitation was done. Bob was awaiting him at the gate, and conducted him around to the back of the big square house. Ned stared in surprise. The tangle of trees and vines and shrubbery had been trimmed to orderly neatness, the long, unkempt grass had been shorn to a yellow, but respectable, turf, and the old arbor showed new strips where Thomas, the Starlings' man, had been at work on the decrepit frame. Near at hand lay piles of cedar and hemlock branches.

"Dad got a couple of the men to cut those down near the tunnel and haul them up here." Bob explained. "Thomas is going to help us put them up. He made a peachy job of the garden, didn't he?"

"You bet!" responded Laurie, heartily. "I wouldn't have known the place! I say, Bob, this arbor's longer than I thought it was."

"Forty feet, about. Why?"

"I only ordered six tables and a dozen chairs from the caterer," answered Laurie, dubiously. "Guess they aren't enough; but he's charging twenty-five cents apiece for them—"

"Twenty-five cents for a table? Isn't that dirt-cheap?"

"We're only renting them, you idiot!"

"Oh, I see. Well, six is enough, I guess; you don't want to crowd them. Now let's get busy with the green stuff. I'll yell down cellar for Thomas. There's a ball of twine, and I've got two hammers and a lot of tacks on the side porch. You take your coat off and I'll—"

"We'll have to have a step-ladder, Bob!"

"There's a short ladder right beside you. Be right back."

Laurie sat down on a wheelbarrow, after removing his coat and folding back the sleeves of his shirt, and looked around him. The garden was fairly large— larger in appearance since the clutter of shrubbery along the sides had been cleared away. Along the School Park edge ran a tall hedge of lilac bushes. At the back was the high board fence, painted dark brown, that separated the garden from the Widow Deane's humble property. On the other side was a rusty ornamental iron fence, mostly hidden by vines. Broad walks, in spite of Thomas's efforts rather overrun with weeds, surrounded the central plot of ancient turf, and another ran straight down the middle of the garden, connecting with the arbor. Wires were to be strung from the trees and across to the arbor, and Chinese lanterns hung thereon. Laurie, half closing his eyes, sought to visualize the place as it would appear on Saturday. He did want the affair to be a success, both financial and artistic, both on account of the school and—well, for the honor of the Turners! While he was musing, two things happened simultaneously: Bob and Thomas appeared from the house, and a familiar voice came to him from the opposite direction.

"Nod!" called the voice. "Nod, will you please come here a moment?"

Laurie's eyes sought the board fence. Over the top of it appeared the head and shoulders of Polly. He left the wheelbarrow and hurried through the arbor and down the walk beyond. Polly's face indicated distress, whether mental or physical Laurie couldn't determine. But Polly's first words explained.

"I can't stay here l-long," she said. "I—I'm just hanging by my elbows. I cl-climbed up on a board, and it's fallen down!"

"I'll get you a ladder!" cried Laurie, gallantly.

"N-no, never mind. I'm going to drop in a s-second. I just want to ask you what Brown's color is. Nettie Blanchard is going to be Brown and—"

"Why, brown, of course!"

"Oh!" There was the sound of desperate scraping against the farther side of the fence, and Polly's countenance became fairly convulsed with the effort of holding herself in sight. "Oh! She said it was pur-pur—"

Polly disappeared. There was a thud from the next yard.

"Purple!" The word floated across to him, muffled but triumphant.

"Are you hurt, Polly?" he called anxiously.

"Not a bit," was the rueful response, "but I'm afraid the day-lilies are!" Then she laughed merrily. "Thanks, Nod! I didn't think Nettie was right. She loves purple, you see!"

"Does she? Well, say, maybe she can be Williams. We weren't going to have Williams, but its color is purple, I think, and if she is going to be disappointed—"

"She will look very well indeed in brown," came from the other side in judicial tones; "and if we begin making changes, half the girls will want to be something they aren't. Why, Pearl Fayles begged to be some girls' college neither Mae nor I had ever heard of, just so she could wear lavender and pale lemon!"

"Well, all right," laughed Laurie. "She'd better stick to Brown—and brown! Good-by, Polly. I'll drop in after a while and find out how things are getting on."

He turned to find Bob viewing him quizzically from the end of the arbor, swinging a hammer in each hand. "Of course it's all right, I dare say," he announced, "but I *thought* you came here to fix up the arbor. Instead of that I find you talking to girls over the fence!"

"There's only one girl," replied Laurie, with dignity, "and we were talking business."

"Oh, of course! Sorry I interrupted."

"You needn't be, and you didn't. Quit grinning like a simpleton and give me a hammer!"

"Right-o! Come on, Thomas! It's quite all right now!"

An hour later their task was done, and well done, and they viewed it with approval. To be honest, the major part of the work had been performed by the faithful Thomas, although it is not to be denied that both Laurie and Bob toiled conscientiously. Before they were through approving the result from various angles, Bob's father joined them. Mr. Starling was an older edition of Bob—a tall, straight, lean-visaged man of forty-two or -three, with the complexion of one who had lived an outdoor life. He had a deep, pleasant voice and a quiet manner not fully in accord with a pair of keen eyes and a firm mouth.

"I'd call that a good piece of work, boys," he said, as he joined them. "And right up to specifications, too. Those paper lanterns come yet, Bob?"

"No, sir; I haven't seen them."

"Lanterns, Mr. Starling?" asked Laurie. "Do you mean Chinese lanterns? We've ordered a lot from the caterer, sir."

"Tell him you won't need them, then. I've got a hundred coming up from the city, Turner. They ought to be here, too. Thomas, call up the express company and ask about them."

"That's very kind, sir," said Laurie, "but you needn't have done it. You— you're doing *everything*!"

"Nonsense! Bob and I want to do our part, of course. Well, this wilderness certainly looks different, doesn't it? That reminds me, Bob; the agent writes me that we may 'make such improvements to the property as we desire.' So, as I consider the absence of that arbor an improvement, I guess you can pull it down any time you like. I'm going to have a cup of tea, Turner. Will you join me? I believe there will be cakes, too."

Laurie found Ned in rather a low frame of mind when he got back to Number 16 a half-hour before supper-time. Ned was hunched over a Latin book and each hand held a firm grip on his hair. At Laurie's arrival he merely grunted.

"Where does it pain you most?" asked Laurie, solicitously, subsiding into a chair with a weary sigh. Ned's mood was far from flippant. He rewarded the other with a scowl, and bent his gaze on the book again. "Want to hear the latest news from the front?" persisted Laurie.

"No, I don't!" his brother growled. "I've had all the news I can stand. Smug says that if I don't get this rotten stuff by nine to-night, and make a perfect showing to-morrow, he will can me!"

"Mr. Cornish said that?" gasped Laurie. "What do you know about that? Why, I thought he was a gentleman!"

"He's a—a brute! I can't learn the old stuff! And I have a hunch that Mulford means to give me a try in the Loring game Saturday. And if I don't get this, Cornish will fix it so I can't play. He as good as said so."

"Didn't you tell him you'd been busy with the fête and everything?"

"Of course I did. Much he cared! Just made a rotten pun. Said I'd better keep my own fate in mind. Puns are fearfully low and vulgar!"

"Aren't they? How much of that have you got?"

"Six pages. I—I've sort of neglected it the last two days. Some fellows can fake through, but I don't have any luck. He's always picking on me."

Laurie whistled expressively. "Six pages! Well, never say die, partner. We'll get down to supper early, and that'll give us two hours before nine."

"Us?" questioned Ned, hopefully.

"Sure. I'll give you a hand. As the well-known proverb so wisely remarks, two heads are the shortest way home."

Ned grinned, and stopped tormenting his hair. "Honest? That's mighty decent, Laurie. I'll do as much for you some day."

"Hope you won't have to. Wash your dirty face and let's beat it!"

At half-past nine a more cheerful and much relieved Ned returned from the hall master's study. "All right," he announced to an anxious Laurie. "He was rather decent, too. Said he guessed that, in view of the manifold affairs engaging my attention just now,—you know the crazy way he talks,—he wouldn't demand too much from me. Reckon he means to let me down easy to-morrow, eh?"

"Maybe, partner, and maybe not. Take my advice and, in the words of the Scouts, be prepared!"

Friday was a hectic day for Laurie and all others concerned with the fête. Difficulties that had remained in ambush all the week sprang out and confronted them at the last moment. Half a dozen things had been forgotten, and every member of the committee sought to exonerate himself. Tempers were short and the meeting in Dan Whipple's room at nine o'clock was far from harmonious. All went to bed that night firmly convinced that the affair was doomed to be a flat failure. And, to add to that conviction, the night sky was overcast and an unsympathetic easterly wind was blowing. Ned, conscious of having imposed too many duties on Laurie, was grouchy and silent; and Laurie, convinced that he had been made a "goat" of, and that Ned was secretly blaming him for mistakes and omissions that were no fault of his, retired in high dudgeon.

And yet, the morning dawned fair and warm, with an almost cloudless blue sky over the world, and life looked very different indeed. Ned arose whistling, and Laurie somehow knew that everything would be all right. Fortunately, they had but two recitations on Saturday, and in consequence there remained to them three whole hours before dinner to devote to the affairs of the entertainment. They were busy hours, you may be sure. If Ned hurried downtown once, he hurried there half a dozen times; while Laurie, seated beside the driver of a rickety express-wagon, rounded up all kinds of things, from the platform at the field-house to the cakes at Miss Comfort's. Dinner brought a respite; but as soon as it was over, Laurie was back on the job, while Ned joined the football-players.

Of course, what the Hillman's School football team should have done that afternoon was to score a decisive victory over the visiting eleven. What it did do was to get thoroughly worsted. Loring was something of a surprise, with a heavier line and a faster bunch of backs than Hillman's had expected. And Loring knew a lot of football, and proved the fact early in the game. At half-past two, by which time the second period was half over, the result was a foregone conclusion. Loring had scored two touch-downs and as many goals therefrom, and the Blue had never once threatened the adversary's last white line. Gains through the opponent were infrequent and short, even Pope, who could generally be depended on to tear off a few yards when the worst came to the worst, failing dismally.

In mid-field, Mason and Slavin made some stirring advances around the Loring wings, and there were several successful forward passes to the home team's credit; but, once past Loring's thirty-yard line, Hillman's seemed powerless. The third quarter went scoreless, and in the fourth, realizing doubtless that defeat was certain, Coach Mulford used his substitutes lavishly. Ned made his first appearance on the big team in that period, taking Mason's place for some eight of the fifteen minutes. He did neither better nor worse than the other second- and third-string fellows, perhaps—although, when Pope was taken out and Deering substituted at full-back, he did his share of the punting and performed very creditably. But that fourth period gave Loring an opportunity to add to her score, and she seized it. Even with several substitutes in her own line-up, she was still far better than Hillman's, and a goal from the field and, in the last few moments of the game, a third touch-down, resulted.

The Blue fought desperately and gamely with her back to the wall, in an effort to stave off that last score; but eventually Holmes, who had taken Kewpie's place at center, weakened, and the Loring back piled through. The final score was 23 to 0, and what two hours before had been looked on as a victory or, at the worst, a tie, had become a cataclysm! Humiliated, if not disgraced, the home-team players trailed to the field-house with hanging heads, averting their eyes from the sight of Loring's triumphal march around the gridiron.

CHAPTER XIV
THE FETE

Behold Fairyland!

Well, at least an excellent imitation of what Fairyland must look like. Overhead, a clear, star-sprinkled sky; below, scores of gaily-hued lanterns shedding their soft glow over a charming scene. Through the side gate, please, on School Park. Twenty-five cents to the boy on duty there, and you are inside, with the manifold attractions awaiting you. On three sides of the transformed garden are the college booths, each decked with bunting and flags of appropriate colors, and each presided over by a patriotically attired young lady who will gladly, nay, eagerly, sell you almost anything from a cake of soap ("Donated by the Town Square Pharmacy, H. J. Congreve, Prop'r.") to a knitted sweater or a gingham house-dress ("Compliments of The New York Store, High Class Dry Goods"). Near at hand, Yale is represented by Miss Polly Deane, capped and aproned in blue, her eyes sparkling and her voice sweetly insistent: "Won't you buy something, please, sir? Post-cards, two for five! These pictures are only fifty cents, all beautifully framed and ready for hanging! Can I sell you something, ma'am?"

Beyond, gay with orange and black, is the Princeton booth; and still beyond, Dartmouth and Columbia and California; and then, a blur of brilliant crimson through the leafage, Harvard. And so on all around the garden, with merry voices sounding above the chatter of the throng that moves here and there. Down the center of Fairyland runs a leafy tunnel from within which blue and red and yellow and green rays twinkle. There, under the hanging lanterns, little tables and chairs are dotted on the gravel, and half a dozen aproned youths are busy bearing, not always without mishap, plates of salad and rolls and dishes of ice-cream and cake. Close to the back of the house is a platform illumined by a row of electric lights, the one glaring spot in the area of soft radiance.

"How's it going?" asked a heavily-built youth of a slimmer one who had paused at the entrance to the arbor.

"Hello, Kewpie! Oh, bully, so far. We took in eighty-four dollars this afternoon, and we'll do at least twice as well to-night. They're still coming. Have you seen Whipple anywhere?"

"Yes, a minute ago, down at the Pennsylvania booth. She's a mighty pretty girl, too, Nod. I bought a pocket-knife of her for a quarter, and got stung; but I don't mind. I'm going back to get another pretty soon. When do I have to sing again?"

"You follow Wilson's clog-dance. We're switching you and Cheesman, Kewpie. His stuff is corking, but it's pretty high-brow, and we thought you'd better bring up the end and make the audience feel cheerful."

"All right; but it won't feel very cheerful if those orchestra guys don't do better than they did this afternoon. They were four or five notes behind me once! Nid said you had a new stunt this evening—something you left out this afternoon."

"Yes; we couldn't work it in daylight very well. It ought to go fine to-night, though."

"What is it?"

"You wait and see. I've got to find Whipple. Say, if you see Ned, tell him I'll be at the platform in five minutes and want him to meet me there. Everybody keeps getting lost here!"

On the way past the arbor, Laurie ran into George Watson, returning across lots balancing a couple of plates in one hand and holding a large slab of cake in the other, from which he nibbled as he went. "Hello!" he said, none too distinctly. "I've been looking for you."

"Wanted to bring me refreshments, I suppose."

George looked at the empty plates, laughed, and shook his head. "Not exactly. I've been feeding Cornell. Somebody ought to take eats to those girls, Nod; they're starving!"

"All right; you do it."

"What do you think I am? A millionaire? I bought Mae a salad and an ice-cream, and I'm about broke. Lend me a half, will you? Thanks. Want an ice-cream? I'll treat."

"No, thanks. Have you seen Dan Whipple?"

"Sure! He's over at the Pennsylvania booth, buying it out! Say, everything's going great, isn't it? Couldn't have had a finer evening, either, what? Well, see you later. I'm hungry!" And George continued his way to the house, where Miss Tabitha, surrounded by willing and hungry helpers, presided sternly, but most capably, over the refreshments.

At eight o'clock the boy on duty at the entrance estimated the attendance as close to two hundred, which, added to the eighty-six paid admissions before supper, brought the total close to the first estimate of three hundred. It is safe to say that every Hillman's boy attended the fête either in the afternoon or evening, and that most of the faculty came and brought Mrs. Faculty— when there was a Mrs. Faculty. Doctor Hillman was spied by Laurie purchasing a particularly useless and unlovely article in burnt wood from the auburn-haired Miss Hatch. Every one seemed to be having a good time, and the only fly in the ointment of the committee was the likelihood that the refreshments would be exhausted far too soon.

The Weather Man had kindly provided an evening of exceptional warmth, with scarcely enough breeze to sway the paper lanterns that glowed from end to end of the old garden, an evening so warm that ice-cream was more in demand than sandwiches or salad; and fortunately so, since ice-cream was the one article of refreshment that could be and was replenished. If, said Ned, folks would stick to ice-cream and go light on the other refreshments, they might get through. To which Laurie agreed, and Ned hied him to the telephone and ordered another freezer sent up.

At a few minutes after eight the Banjo and Mandolin Club took possession of the chairs behind the platform and dashed into a military march. Following that, six picked members of the Gymnastic Club did some very clever work, and Cheesman, a tall and rather soulful-looking upper middler, sang two ballads very well indeed, and then, as an encore, quite took the joy out of life with "Suwanee River"! Little Miss Comfort, present through the courtesy of the Committee on Arrangements, sniffled quite audibly, but was heard to declare that "it was just too sweet for anything!" A rather embarrassed junior attempted some card tricks that didn't go very well, and then Wilson, garbed more or less in the character of an Irish gentleman returning from Donnybrook Fair, and swinging a shillaly, did some jig-dancing that was really clever and won much applause.

There was a brief unofficial intermission while three anxious committee members made search for Kewpie Proudtree. He was presently discovered consuming his fourth plate of ice-cream in the seclusion of the side porch, and was haled away, protesting, to the platform. In spite of what may seem an over-indulgence in refreshment, Kewpie was in excellent voice and a jovial mood, and sang four rollicking songs in a manner that captured his audience. In fact, long after Kewpie had vanished from the public gaze and returned to his ice-cream, the audience still demanded more.

Its attention was eventually captured, however, by Dan Whipple, who announced importantly that it gave him much pleasure to say that, at a great expense, the committee had secured as an added attraction the world-famed Signor Duodelli, who, with their kind permission, would exhibit for their pleasure and astoundment his miraculous act known as the Vanishing Man, as performed before the crowned heads of Europe, to the bewilderment and applause of all beholders. "Ladies and gentlemen, Signor Duodelli!"

The Signor had a noticeable likeness to Lew Cooper, in spite of his gorgeous mustache and flowing robe of red and purple cheese-cloth. Yet it might not have been Lew, for his manner was extremely foreign and his gestures and the few words he used in directing the arranging of his "properties" were unmistakably Latin. The properties consisted of a kitchen chair, a threefold screen covered with black baize, and a coil of rope. There was also in evidence a short wand, but the Signor held that in his hand, waving it around most eloquently. The audience laughed and applauded and waited patiently until the chair had been placed exactly to the Signor's liking, close to the back of the platform, and the screen beside it. Previously several of the lights had been put out, and those that remained threw their glare on the front of the stage, leaving the back, while discernible, less in evidence.

"Now," announced the Signor, narrowly escaping from falling off the platform as he tripped over his robe, "I aska da some one coma up and giva da help. Any one I aska. You, Signor, maybe, eh?" The magician pointed his wand at Mr. Cornish, in the front of the clustered audience; but the gentleman laughingly declined. The Signor seemed disappointed. "No-o-o? You no geta da hurt. Some one else, eh?" He looked invitingly around, and a small junior, urged by his companions, struggled to the front. Unfortunately for his ambitions to pose in the lime-light, the Signor's glance had moved to another quarter, and, ere the junior could get his attention, a volunteer appeared from the semi-obscurity of the kitchen porch. He was peculiarly attired, wearing a simple white garment having a strong resemblance to the old-fashioned night-shirt, that covered him completely from neck to ankles. He was bareheaded, revealing the fact that his locks were red-brown in hue.

"Ah!" exclaimed the Signor, delightedly. "You will helpa me, *si?* Right thisa way, Signor. I thanka you!"

"That's one of the Turner fellows," muttered a boy, while the small junior and his companions called "Fake!" loudly. However, the good-natured laughter of the audience drowned the accusation, and some two hundred pairs of eyes watched amusedly and expectantly while, with the assistance of two other volunteers, the youth in the white robe was tied securely to the chair.

"Maka him tight," directed the Signor, enthusiastically, waving his wand. "Pulla da knot. Ha, thata da way! Good! Signors, I thanka you!"

The two who had tied the victim to the chair retired from the platform. The Signor seized the screen and opened it wide and turned it around and closed it and turned it again.

"You seea?" he demanded. "There is nothing that deceive! Now, then, I placea da screen so!" He folded it around the boy and the chair, leaving only the side away from the audience uncovered. He drew away the width of the platform, and, "Music, ifa you please," he requested. The orchestra, whose members had moved their chairs to one side, struck up a merry tune, and the Signor, folding his arms, bent a rapt gaze on the blank, impenetrable blackness of the screen. A brief moment passed. Then the Signor bade the music cease, took a step forward, and pointed to the screen.

"Away!" he cried, and swung his arm in a half-circle, his body following with a weird flaring of his brilliant robes until, with outstretched finger, he faced the audience. "Ha! He come! Thisa way, Signor! Comea quick!"

As one man the audience turned and followed the pointing finger. Through the deserted arbor came a boy in a white garment. He pushed his way through the throng and jumped to the stage. As he did so, the Signor whisked aside the screen. There was the chair empty, and there was the rope dangling from it, twisted and knotted.

A moment of surprised silence gave place to hearty applause. Theoretically it might have been possible for the boy in the chair to vanish from behind the screen, reach the farther end of the garden, and run back into sight; but actually, as the audience realized on second thought, it couldn't possibly have been done in the few seconds, surely not more than ten, that had elapsed between the placing of the screen and the appearance of the boy behind them. And then, how had he got himself free from the rope? An audience likes to be puzzled, and this one surely was. The garden hummed with conjecture and discussion. There were some there who could have explained the seeming phenomenon, but they held their counsel.

Meanwhile, on the platform the Signor was modestly bowing alternately to the audience and to his subject, the latter apparently no worse for his magic transposition. And the orchestra again broke into its interrupted melody. The applause became insistent, but Signor Duodelli, perhaps because his contract with the committee called for no further evidence of his powers, only bowed and bowed and at last disappeared into the obscurity of the shadows. Whereupon the Banjo and Mandolin Club moved into the house, and presently the strains of a one-step summoned the dancers to the big drawing-room.

Laurie, unconsciously rubbing a wrist, smiled as he listened to the comments of the dissolving audience. "Well, but there's no getting around the fact that it was the same boy," declared a pompous little gentleman to his companion. "Same hair and eyes and everything! Couldn't be two boys as much alike, eh? Not possibly! Very clever!"

Laurie chuckled as he made his way to Polly's booth. That young lady looked a little tired, and, by the same token, so did the Yale booth! Only a bare dozen framed pictures and a small number of post-cards remained of her stock. "Don't you think I've done awfully well?" asked Polly, a trifle pathetically. She seemed to need praise, and Laurie supplied it.

"Corking, Polly," he assured her. "I guess you've sold more than any of the others, haven't you?"

"N-no, I guess some of the others have done better, Nod; but I think they had more attractive articles, don't you? Anyhow, I've taken in twelve dollars and thirty cents since supper, and I made four dollars and eighty-five cents this afternoon; only I must have dropped a dime somewhere, for I'm ten cents short. Or perhaps someone didn't give me the right amount."

"Why, that's seventeen dollars!" exclaimed Laurie. "I didn't think you had anywhere near seventeen dollars' worth of things here, Polly!"

"Oh, I didn't! Not nearly! Why, if I'd sold things at the prices marked on them, Nod, I wouldn't have had more than half as much! But lots of folks *wanted* to pay more, and I let them. Mr. Conklin, the jeweler, bought a picture, one of the funny landscapes with the frames that didn't fit at the corners, and he said it was ridiculous to sell it for a quarter, and he gave me a dollar for it. Then he held the picture up and just laughed and laughed at it! I guess he just wanted to spend his money, don't you? You know, Ned said we were to get as much as we could for things, so I usually added ten cents to the price that was marked on them—sometimes more, if a person looked extravagant. One lady came back and said she'd paid twenty-five cents for a picture and it was marked fifteen on the back. I said I was sorry she was dissatisfied and I'd be very glad to buy it back from her for twenty."

Laurie laughed. "What did she say to that?" he asked.

"She said if I wanted it bad enough to pay twenty cents for it she guessed it was worth twenty-five, and went off and didn't come back." Polly laughed and then sighed. "I'm awfully tired. Doesn't that music sound lovely? Do you dance?"

Laurie shook his head. "No; but, say, if you want to go in there, I'll watch the booth for you."

Polly hesitated. "It's funny you don't," she said. "Don't you like it?"

It was Laurie's turn to hesitate. "No, not much. I never have danced. It—it seems sort of silly." He looked at Polly doubtfully. Although he wouldn't have acknowledged it, he was more than half sorry that dancing was not included among his accomplishments.

"It isn't silly at all," asserted Polly, almost indignantly. "You ought to learn. Mae could teach you to one-step in no time at all!"

"I guess that's about the way I'd do it," answered Laurie, sadly—"in no time at all! Don't you—couldn't *you* teach a fellow?"

"I don't believe so. I never tried to teach any one. Besides, Mae dances lots better than I do. She put the things she had left on Grace Boswell's booth and went inside the minute the music started. She wanted me to come, but I thought I shouldn't," added Polly, virtuously.

"You go ahead now," urged Laurie. "I'll stay here till you come back. It isn't fair for you girls to miss the dancing. Besides, I guess there won't be much more sold now. Folks have begun to go, some of them, and most of the others are inside."

Polly looked toward the house. Through the big wide-open windows the lilting music of a waltz floated out. The Banjo and Mandolin Club was really doing very well to-night. Polly sighed once and looked wistful. Then she shook her head. "Thanks, Nod," she said, "but I guess I'll stay here. Some one *might* come."

"What do you care? You don't own 'em! Anyway, I guess I could sell a post-card if I had to!"

"You'd have trouble selling any of those pictures," laughed Polly. "Aren't they dreadful? Where did they come from?"

"Pretty fierce," Laurie agreed. "They came from the Metropolitan Furniture Store. The man dug them out of a corner in the cellar. I guess he'd had them for years! Anyway, there was enough dust on them to choke you. He seemed awfully tickled when we agreed to take them and let him alone!"

"I should think he might have! We girls agreed to buy things from each other, just to help, but the only things they bought from me were post-cards!" Polly laughed as though at some thought; and Laurie, who had elevated himself to an empty corner of the booth and was swinging his feet against the blue draping in front, looked inquiringly. "I was just thinking about the boys," explained Polly.

"What about them? What boys do you mean?" Laurie asked coldly.

"The high school boys. They're awfully peeved because we girls took part in this, and not one of them has been here, I guess."

"Cheeky beggars," grumbled Laurie. "Guess we can do without them, though. Here comes Bob's father."

Mr. Starling was bent on a most peculiar mission. Laurie and Polly watched him stop at the next booth and engage in conversation. Then a fat pocket-book was produced, a bill was tendered, and Mr. Starling strolled on. At the Yale booth he stopped again.

"Well, Turner," he greeted, "this affair looks like a huge success, doesn't it? Why aren't you young folks inside there, dancing?"

"I don't dance, sir," answered Laurie, somewhat to his chagrin in a most apologetic tone. "And Polly thinks she ought to stand by the ship. This is Polly Deane, Mr. Starling."

Bob's father shook hands cordially across the depleted counter and assured its proprietor that he was very glad indeed to make her acquaintance. Then he added: "But you don't seem to have much left, Miss Polly. Now, I'm a great hand at a bargain. I dare say that if you made me a fair price for what there is here I'd jump at it. What do you say?"

Polly apparently didn't know just what to say for a minute, and her gaze sought counsel of Laurie.

"If you ask me," laughed the latter, "I'd say fifty cents was a big price for the lot!"

"You're not in charge," said Mr. Starling, almost severely. "I'm sure the young lady has better business ability. Suppose you name a price, Miss Polly."

"We-ell—" Polly did some mental arithmetic, and then, doubtfully: "A dollar and a half, sir," she said.

"Done!" replied Mr. Starling. He drew forth a two-dollar bill. "There you are! Just leave the things where they are. I'll look after them later. Now you youngsters go in and dance. What's this? Change? My dear young lady, don't you know that change is never given at an affair of this kind? I really couldn't think of taking it. It—it's a criminal offense!" And Mr. Starling nodded and walked away.

"By Jove, he's a brick!" exclaimed Laurie, warmly. "Look, he's doing the same thing everywhere!"

"I know," answered Polly, watching. "It's just dear of him, isn't it? But, Nod, *what* do you suppose he will do with these awful pictures?"

"The same thing he will do with that truck he's buying now," was the laughing reply. "He will probably put them in the furnace!"

"Well," said Polly, after a moment, "I suppose we might as well go inside, don't you? We can look on, anyway, and"—with a stifled sigh—"I'd 'most as lief look on as dance."

Laurie followed, for the second time in his life wishing that the Terpsichorean art had been included in his education!

CHAPTER XV
NED HAS AN IDEA

"Three hundred and thirty-three dollars and eighty-five cents," said Ned, in very satisfied tones. "We took in three hundred and sixty-three five, but we had twenty-nine twenty to come out for expenses. Not so bad, what?"

"But something tells me," answered Laurie, mournfully, "that if all our expenses were deducted we'd have less than that. You see," he explained to Polly, "I lost the piece of paper that I set down the money I paid out on, and I just had to guess what it all came to, because I'd never had time to add it up."

"I dare say you guessed enough," replied Ned, untroubled.

"I dare say I didn't, then!" was the indignant response. "If I did, where's all the money I had when I started? I've got a dollar and ninety cents left, and I had over four dollars when you roped me in on the thing! I'm more than two dollars shy, I tell you!"

"Oh, well, it's gone for a worthy cause," laughed Ned.

"Maybe," Laurie grumbled, "but I notice that none of yours has gone that way. You always made me pay for everything!"

"Well, I think you did it beautifully," said Polly. "I never suspected you'd make so much!"

They were in the little garden behind the shop. It was the second day after the fête, and the bell in the Congregational church tower had just struck two. There was a perceptible nip in the air to-day, and the flowers in the border showed blackened leaves, while the nasturtiums were frankly limp and lifeless. But here in the sunshine it was warm enough, and Laurie, spurning the bench, was seated tailor fashion on the yellowing turf. Polly had stated her absolute certitude that he would catch cold, but Laurie derided the idea.

"We're awfully much obliged to you girls," said Ned. "We wouldn't have done nearly so well if you hadn't helped. I think the committee ought to give you a—a vote of thanks or something."

"Oh, we all loved it!" Polly assured him earnestly. "We had heaps of fun. Why, I wouldn't have missed that disappearing trick for anything. I was positively thrilled when Laurie came running up the garden!"

The boys' laughter interrupted, and Polly looked puzzled.

"That wasn't Laurie," explained Ned. "That was me."

"But I was sure you were the one in the chair! And if you were in the chair, how could you—"

"I wasn't, though. That was Laurie."

Polly sighed despairingly. "I'll never get so I can tell you apart," she said; "unless I hear you talk, that is! I don't see yet how it was done. Won't you please tell me?"

"It was as easy as easy," replied Ned. "You see, the way I planned it first—"

"The way *who* planned it?" inquired Laurie.

"Well, the way *we* planned it, then."

"Hold on! Whose idea was it in the first place, partner?"

"Oh, don't be so fussy! Anyway, you couldn't have done it without me!"

"I never said I could. But you've got a lot of cheek to talk about the way *you*—"

Polly clapped her hands to her ears. "I'm not being told how it was done, and I do want to know. Go on, Ned."

"Well, it was done like this. You see, Laurie was tied to the chair, and I was hiding out at the other end of the garden. Then Lew Cooper put the screen around the chair." Polly nodded. "Then I started toward the platform, and every one turned to look at me." Polly nodded again. "Well, right behind the platform was the bulkhead door into the cellar. When Cooper shouted to me to come on, two fellows who were on the stairs waiting pushed the door open, grabbed Laurie, chair and all, and whisked him down cellar. Then they put another chair, just like the first one, behind the screen, and when Cooper pulled the screen away, there it was, just as if Laurie had somehow untied himself and—and vanished! Of course, if any one had been looking at the screen instead of at me just then, he might have seen what was going on, although it was pretty dark behind there and he mightn't have. Anyway, no one was, I guess. The trick depended on the—the faint similarity between us. Lots of fellows who knew us were on to it, but the folks from the village were puzzled for fair!"

"Indeed they were," agreed Polly. "They just couldn't understand it at all!"

"It would have been better," mused Laurie, "if we could have taken the screen away and showed the empty chair before Ned came into sight; but there didn't seem to be any way of doing that. We had to have the people looking the other way, and we had to work quick. As it was, I was half killed, for Wainwright and Plummer were in such a hurry to get the other chair up there that they just dumped me on my back! And then they ran upstairs through the kitchen to see the end of it, and I was kicking around down there for five minutes!"

"Well," said Ned, a few minutes later, "I'm not finding out what to do with this." He opened one hand and exposed some bills and two ten-cent pieces folded into a wad. "Your mother says she won't take it, Polly—that she didn't understand we were going to pay her for the cream-puffs. Gee, we wouldn't have thought of asking her to make them for nothing!"

Polly nodded sympathetically. "Mother says, though, that the boys bring so much trade to her that it's only fair for her to help them."

"That's poppy-cock!" said Laurie. "Seven dollars and twenty cents is a lot of money. Look here; don't you think she ought to take it, Polly?"

Polly was silent a moment. Then she nodded affirmatively. "Yes, I do," she said frankly. "She really needs the money, Ned. I wouldn't tell any one else, but we're just frightfully hard up, and I wouldn't be a bit surprised if Mother had to give up here before very long."

"Give up!" exclaimed Ned. "You mean—go away?"

"Yes. You see, she doesn't make very much money in the store; nothing like she used to before the war sent prices so high. And then, what with taxes and water and light, and the interest on the mortgage, why, it hardly pays. Just the same, if she says she won't take the money, Ned, why, I guess she won't, and that's all there is to it. But she ought to!"

"Can't she charge more for things?" asked Laurie. "Everyone else does nowadays. That bake-shop down on Hudson Street gets eight cents for cream-puffs and éclairs, and you sell them for six."

"I know; but Mama says six cents is enough and that the boys oughtn't to have to pay any more. And lots of things she sells for hardly any more than she used to before prices advanced. Why, I have to watch all the time; and when bills come in for things, I have to compare them with what we're getting for them, and lots of times I find that Mama's been selling for less than what she's paid! She just won't be a profiteer, she says!"

"Gee! I hope you don't have to shut up," said Laurie. He looked around the little garden. "It—it's such a jolly place! And the house and everything. Gee, that would be a shame!"

Polly sighed while she nodded. "It is nice," she agreed; "but there are so many things that ought to be done! Uncle Peter never would do much for us. He did promise to have the house painted, but he died about a month after that, and so it was never done."

"Suppose he up and died so's he wouldn't have to do it?" inquired Laurie, suspiciously.

Polly shook her head and looked a trifle shocked, until she caught the smile in Ned's eyes.

"It doesn't look as if it would cost much money to paint it," remarked Ned, looking up at the rear of the little two-and-a-half-story building. "It's not much more than a doll's house, anyway. How many rooms are there, Polly?"

"Three upstairs, and then a sort of attic room under the roof; and two downstairs."

"Uh-huh. I just wondered. It wouldn't be much of a trick to paint the outside. Bet you I could do it in a couple of days."

Laurie gasped. "A couple of days! You? How do you get like that? It would take a real painter a week to do it!"

"Maybe; but I'm not a real painter," answered Ned, grinning. He glanced at the crumpled wad in his hand and held it tentatively toward Polly. "Maybe you'd better take charge of this, Polly, until we decide what to do with it."

But Polly put her hands resolutely behind her, and shook her head with decision. "No, Ned, I'd rather not. If Mama says she won't have it, she won't, and you might just as well give it back to the—the fund."

Somewhat to Laurie's surprise, Ned pocketed the money without further protest. "All right," he said. "It's very kind of your mother. We mustn't forget to see that her name's included in the list of those who donated things, Laurie. This week's 'Messenger' is going to tell all about it. Well, I've got to pull my freight. You coming, partner?"

"Yes, I guess so," replied Laurie, without much enthusiasm. "I promised Bob and George to get another fellow and play some tennis this afternoon."

"Gee! it must be great to have nothing to do but play," sighed his brother.

"Huh, any one would think, to hear you talk, that you were working," replied Laurie, crushingly. "All you do is stand around and watch the others."

"Think so?" Ned smiled in a superior way. "You come down this afternoon and see how much standing around I do. Joe Stevenson says I've got to practise goals now. Isn't that the limit?"

"I suppose it pains him to see you loafing," said Laurie. "Anyway, I dare say it'll keep you out of mischief."

Laurie led the way to the back fence, against which leaned a plank with two pieces of wood nailed across it. This afforded a short cut to and from school, and was an idea of Bob's. From the top of the fence they dropped into the shrubbery and then made their way to the side gate.

The arbor had not yet been denuded of its evergreen clothing, and there were other evidences of the recent festival in the shape of crumpled paper napkins lying on the ground. Thomas had taken down the lanterns and was packing them away in their case by the kitchen porch, and the boys called a greeting to him as they passed.

"Bob still mean to make a tennis-court here?" asked Ned, as they went through the gate.

"Yes. He's going to tear down that arbor right away, he says. So far, though, he hasn't found any one to do the work on the court. Every one is busy. I don't believe he will get it done in time to use it this fall."

"Of course he won't. It's nearly November now. Say, you'd better take this money and hand it over to Whipple. You'll see him before I do. And tell him to put Mrs. Deane's name down with the other folks who contributed, will you?"

"All right; but I think it's a shame to let her stand for all those cakes."

"So do I; only—"

"Only what?"

"Maybe we can make it up to her another way. I've got an idea, Laurie."

"I hope it's better than most of 'em. What is it?"

And when Ned had explained it, Laurie considered a long moment and then indorsed it enthusiastically. "That's corking!" he cried. "For once, Ned, the old bean has worked! Only, when could we—"

"Christmas vacation," said Ned. "We won't have much to do then. What do you say?"

"I say that, for the first time in my life, Neddie, I'm proud to acknowledge you as my twin!"

CHAPTER XVI
POLLY TELLS A SPOOK STORY

Assured of sufficient funds to complete its season without financial embarrassment, the Hillman's football team seemed to take a new and firmer grip on things. Practice went well that week, and the players showed vim and snap. Perhaps the colder weather helped, too. The line-up that faced the scrubs on Friday for a short scrimmage was, barring accidents, that which would, four weeks later, start the game against Hillman's old rival, Farview Academy. Farley and White were at the ends, Captain Stevenson and Pringle were the tackles, Emerson and Corson were the guards, and Kewpie Proudtree was at center. Frank Brattle at quarter, Mason and Slavin for halves, and Pope at full-back composed the rest of the team. There were some weak places, to be sure; but, on the whole, Coach Mulford was fairly satisfied that he had the parts for a capable machine.

Ned was still playing on the scrub eleven, and doing rather well. As a punter, at least, he deserved his position at left half, and it might be that he would develop into a fair goal-kicker; for in the last four days, under the tuition of the coach and full-back Pope, he had shown excellent promise. Those morning lessons, now abandoned, had grounded Ned well in the art of toeing the pigskin, and, whatever fame the future might hold for him as punter or drop-kicker or place-kicker, much of the credit would be Kewpie's.

To-day, in the second ten minutes of the scrimmaging,—there was but twenty minutes in all,—Thursby, playing quarter, and probably acting under instructions, gave Ned his first chance to show what he could do in the way of field goals. Unable to reach a point nearer than twenty yards to the school team's goal, Thursby called for "kick formation, Turner back," and Ned went up-field with his heart in his mouth. Although the cross-bar was less than thirty yards from where he took his stand and almost directly in front of him, it looked to Ned to be a woeful distance away and the angle much more severe than it was. But he didn't have much time for reflection, for Thursby called his signal quickly, and the leather came back to him at a good pass, and the school team was crashing through.

Ned always thought that he closed his eyes when he swung his toe against the rebounding ball and trusted to luck, but I doubt it, for the pigskin described a perfect arc and went well and true over the bar, and if Ned had had his eyes closed I don't believe the pigskin would have acted that way at all. Most of the scrub team players thumped him on the back and showed their delight in other ways, for they had not scored on the school team for nearly a week; while, at a little distance, Coach Mulford nodded his head almost imperceptibly. It was too bad Ned didn't see that nod, for it would have pleased him far more than the buffets of his team-mates.

The next day Hillman's made a trip to Warring and played the Lansing team to a standstill, returning with a 22-0 victory tucked under its belt. Ned got into the game for a bare five minutes at the last, as did half a dozen other substitutes; but he was not called on to kick any goals, for which he was at once sorry and glad. To have had the eyes of nearly a thousand persons on him would, he thought, have precluded any possibility of success; but, on the other hand, had he succeeded—He sighed for lost opportunities!

The attendance that afternoon was a matter of great joy to Manager Dave Murray, for Hillman's went home with a neat sum as its share of the day's profits, a sum far larger than he had counted on—large enough, in fact, to make up the difference between the net receipts from the fête and the three hundred and fifty dollars aimed at.

Hillman's good fortune held for another week. There were no accidents during practice; every fellow in the line-up played for all that was in him; and the scrubs took a licking every afternoon. Ned twice more gained glory as a drop-kicker, although on a third occasion he failed lamentably. Unfortunately, neither of his successes brought victory to his team, since the opponents had on each occasion a safe lead in the scoring. Every afternoon, following the scrimmage, Ned was presented by the coach with a nice battle-scarred football, and instructed to go down to the east goal and "put some over." Sometimes Hop Kendrick or Ben Thursby went with him to hold the ball while he tried placement-kicks, and always an unhappy substitute was delegated to retrieve the pigskin for him; but the coach let him pretty much alone, and Pope looked on only occasionally and was surprisingly sparing of comment or advice. And yet, Ned improved, rather to his surprise, since he felt himself neglected and, as he said to Laurie, didn't see how they expected a fellow to learn goal-kicking if they didn't show him a little! But, although he didn't realize it, Ned had reached a point in his development where he was best left to his own devices, and Coach Mulford knew it and forbore to risk confusing him with unnecessary instruction. So Ned pegged away doggedly, and got results, as he considered, in spite of the coach!

Against the Queens Preparatory Institute, which journeyed up from the city on Saturday, the Blue was able to emerge from four grueling fifteen-minute periods with the score 6-6, from the Blue's standpoint a very satisfactory showing, for Q. P. I. was a much-heralded team and had downed stronger elevens than Hillman's. So November began its second week, and cloudy days and not infrequently rainy ones took the place of the sunny weather of October.

Laurie would have been somewhat at a loss for a way in which to spend his afternoons at that time, had it not been for Bob Starling's overmastering desire to build a tennis-court in the garden of the Coventry place. The weather was far too cold for tennis, although now and then he and Bob played George and Lee Murdock, and the wrecking of the old grape-arbor, preparatory to digging up the sod, proved a welcome diversion. Sometimes Thomas took a hand; but Thomas had plenty to do indoors, and the work was accomplished almost wholly by Bob and Laurie, with the occasional moral support of George or Lee.

Usually an hour's labor with hammer or crowbar ended with an adjournment to the Widow Deane's, by way of the back fence, for refreshments. Sometimes it was warm enough to foregather in the little garden behind the shop and, armed with cream-puffs or tarts, spend a jolly half-hour in the society of Polly and Mae. At such times Mrs. Deane, hearing the shouts and laughter, came to the back door and smiled in sympathy.

One glorious afternoon of mingled sunlight and frost there was an excursion afoot out into the country in search of nuts. Polly and Mae and Laurie and George and Bob and Lee formed the party. They carried two baskets, one of which George wore on his head most of the way, to the wonderment of the infrequent passers. Mae knew, or thought she knew, where there were chestnut trees, and led the way for three miles to what is called Two Jug Ridge. The chestnut trees, however, were, according to Laurie, away for the afternoon. They found some hickory nuts, not quite ready to leave their husks, and a few beech-nuts, and after gathering those they sat on a broad, flat boulder and looked down on Orstead and Little Windsor and some twelve miles of the Hudson River, and talked a good deal of nonsense—all except Lee, who went to sleep with his cap pulled over his eyes, and had a cold in his head for days after. George decided that when he was through college and was married, he would come back there and build a bungalow just where they were seated.

"This will do for the front door-step," he expounded, "and over there will be a closed-in porch with an open fireplace and a Gloucester hammock."

"That all you're going to have?" asked Bob. "No kitchen?"

"Oh, there'll be a kitchen, all right, and a dining-room—no, I guess we'll eat on the porch. Wouldn't it be a dandy place, though? Look at the view!"

"Fine," said Laurie, without much enthusiasm, remembering the last uphill mile. "Don't mind if I don't come to see you often, though, do you?"

"Not a bit! Nobody asked you, anyway."

"You could live on nuts," murmured Polly, "and could have shaggy-barks for breakfast and beech-nuts for dinner and—"

"Grape-nuts for supper," said Laurie, coming to the rescue.

"And you could call the place the Squirrel-Cage," suggested Bob.

And that reminded Mae of a story her father had told of a man who had lived in the woods farther down the river some years before, and who ate nothing but nuts and things he found in the forest. "He lived all alone in a little cabin he'd built, and folks said he was a deserter from the army, and—"

"What army?" George asked.

"The Northern Army, of course."

"I thought you might mean the Salvation Army. Then this was quite awhile ago, wasn't it?"

"Of course, stupid! Years and years ago. And finally, when he died, folks found that he wasn't a deserter at all, but a general or a major or something, and they found a prize that the government had given him, some sort of a medal for bravery in battle. Wasn't that sad?"

"Well," replied Laurie, doubtfully, "I suppose it was. I suppose the government would have shown better judgment if they'd given him a bag of nuts. Of course, he couldn't eat that medal!"

"You're horrid! Anyway, it just shows that you mustn't judge folks by—by outward appearances, doesn't it?"

"Rather! I've always said that, too. Take George, for example. Just to look at him, you'd never think he had any sense at all; but at times—"

"Lay off of George," interrupted that young gentleman, threateningly. "If folks judged you by the way you talk, you'd be inside a nice high wall!"

Why the talk should have drifted from there to the subject of ghosts and uncanny happenings isn't apparent, but it did. In the midst of it, Lee gave a tremendous snore that scared both the girls horribly, and sat up suddenly, blinking. "Hello!" he muttered. Then he yawned and grinned foolishly. "Guess I must have dropped off," he said apologetically.

"You didn't," said George. "If you had you'd have waked up quicker! Cut out the chatter; Polly's telling a spook yarn."

Lee gathered up a handful of beech-nuts and was silent except for the sound he made in cracking the shells.

"It isn't much of a story," disclaimed Polly, "but it—it *was* funny. It began just after Mama and I came here. I mean, that was the first time. One night, after we had gone to bed, Mama called me. 'I think there's some one downstairs, Polly,' she whispered. We both listened, and, sure enough, we could hear a sort of tapping sound. It wasn't like footsteps, exactly; more—more hollow, as if it came from a long way off. But it sounded right underneath. We listened a minute or two, and then it stopped and didn't begin again; and presently we lighted a candle and went downstairs, and nobody was there and everything was quite all right. So we thought that perhaps what we'd heard was some one walking along the street.

"We didn't hear it again for nearly two weeks, and then it lasted longer—maybe two minutes. It got louder; and stopped, and began again, and died away; and we sat there and listened, and I thought of ghosts and everything except robbers, because it didn't sound like any one in the store. It was more as if it was some one in the cellar."

"Well, maybe it was," suggested Laurie, when Polly paused.

"That's what we thought, Nod, until we went to see. Then we remembered that there wasn't any cellar!"

"Oh!" said Laurie.

"What happened then?" asked Lee, flicking a shell at George.

"It kept on happening every little while for two years. We got so we didn't think any more about it. Mr. Farmer, the lawyer, said what we heard was probably a rat. But I know very well it wasn't that. It was too regular. It was always just the same each time. At first we could just hear it a little, and then it grew louder and louder, and stopped. And then it began again, loud, and just sort of—of trailed off till you couldn't hear it at all. I suppose we never would have heard it if it hadn't been for Mama not sleeping very well, because it always came after midnight, usually about half-past twelve. After a while I didn't hear it at all, because Mama stopped waking me up."

"Spooks," declared George, with unction. "The house is haunted, Polly."

"Wish I lived there," said Bob eagerly. "I'm crazy about ghosts. They told me that old Coven—I mean your uncle, Polly—haunted the house we're in; but, gee! I've been around at all times of night and never seen a thing! There are lots of jolly, shivery noises—stairs creaking, and woodwork popping, and all that, you know; but nary a ghost. Look here, Polly! Let me sit down in the store some night, will you? I'd love to!"

"You've got funny ideas of fun," murmured George.

"Oh, but it's gone now," said Mae. "Hasn't it, Polly? You haven't heard the noise for a long time, have you?"

"No, not for—oh, two years, I think. At least, that's what Mama says. Maybe, though, she sleeps better and doesn't hear things."

"I guess Mr. What's-his-name was right," said Lee. "It was probably a rat, or a family of rats."

"Rats wouldn't make the same sound every time," scoffed Laurie.

"They might. Trained rats might. Maybe they escaped from a circus."

"And maybe you escaped from an asylum," responded Laurie, getting up. "Let's take him home before he gets violent."

CHAPTER XVII
LAURIE MAKES A PROTEST

The football team continued to add victories, and as the fateful 20th of November approached enthusiasm grew until, after the Whittier game, which Hillman's won by a field goal in the final hectic two minutes, it became more a furore than enthusiasm. Ned, by that time, had settled down to a realization that, no matter what progress he made this fall, no matter how adept he became at kicking a football down the field or over the cross-bar, he would not make the first team; that, in short, he was being educated as next year material. There was no injustice in this, and he realized it; for, aside from his proficiency as a kicker, he was not in the class with the school team backs. He couldn't worm his way through a hole in the opposing line the way Slavin could, nor smash through the defense the way Mason did, nor dodge and side-step in a broken field like Pope. Once going, Ned was rather hard to stop, for he displayed some of the slippery qualities of an eel; but it took him ten yards to get his speed up, and the opponents had a discouraging way of getting through and flooring him before the tenth yard was won! But he had grown to love the game, and no one toiled more conscientiously. There were times when Laurie devoutly wished that Ned hadn't taken up the game, for after a half-hour of Ned's chatter Laurie found the subject of football a trifle dull.

On the Wednesday before the Farview contest the Orstead High School team came over for a practice game. At least, Hillman's called it a practice game and considered it such; but High School had blood in her eye and was secretly determined to wreak all the vengeance possible. Once a year, for the space of some three hours, Orstead High School swore allegiance to Hillman's and turned out at the field and rooted valiantly for the Blue while she battled with Farview. But all the rest of the time she was frankly hostile and derisive. This Wednesday afternoon the hostility was apparent from the first. More than a hundred boys and a scattering of girls followed their team to the Hillman's field and demanded revenge for the early-season defeat, while the High School team, which had passed through a rather successful season and was not at all the aggregation that the Blue had beaten 10 to 7, started right out after it.

Coach Mulford began with his first-string players, and against them High School was not dangerous, although there were anxious moments. The second period ended with the score 7—0 in Hillman's favor, only a fumble by Slavin on High School's eight yards saving the visitor from a second touch-down. When the third quarter began, Coach Mulford put in nearly a new eleven, only Kewpie Proudtree, Farley, Mason, and Pope remaining over. Perhaps the High School coach had talked new strength and determination into his charges during the intermission, for the visitors started in on the second half in whirlwind fashion. The Blue kicked off, and High School's quarter got the ball on his twenty-five-yard line and scampered back to the thirty-five before he was laid low by Farley, the Blue's left end. From there, with fierce slams at Hillman's right and two short forward passes over the center of the line, High School reached the opponent's thirty-two. There an off-side penalty set her back, and, after two attempts at rushing that produced but three yards, she kicked to the five-yard line. Kendrick fumbled the catch, but recovered and was downed on his ten. Pope punted on second down to mid-field, and from there High School started another slashing advance that took her to the thirty-four yards before she was halted.

On the side-lines, the High School supporters were shouting and beseeching and banners were waving deliriously. A tow-haired full-back, who had all along proved the visitor's best ground-gainer, smashed through the Hillman's left for two yards; and then, on fourth down, faking a kick, he set off on a romp around the adversary's right. Lightner, the second-string end, was effectually boxed, and the runner, turning wide, was off down the field at top speed. Only Hop Kendrick stood between him and the goal-line, and Hop waited on the fifteen yards, wary and alert. The tow-haired boy's feint to the right didn't fool him, and when the side-stepping to the left began, Hop was on him with a clean dive and a hard tackle, and the two rolled to earth together. But the ball was on the thirteen yards now, and it was first down for High School, and the latter was not to be denied. A plunge off tackle took the pigskin in front of the goal, though there was no gain. Hillman's piled up an attack at right guard. On third down, High School called for kick formation, and the tow-haired terror dropped back.

From the side of the gridiron, Hillman's rooters chanted: "Block that kick! Block that kick!" But there was no kick to block, for the full-back only backed away a pace or two when the pigskin reached him, and then tossed to the corner of the field and to the eager hands of an uncovered right end who had but to make three strides before he was over the line. Hop got him then; but the damage was done, and the visitors lining the gridiron were cheering and cavorting wildly. The kick was from a difficult angle, but the tow-haired player made it, and the score was tied.

The teams changed fields a minute later. Undismayed, Coach Mulford sent in three new substitutes, one of them in place of Pope. Hillman's got the ball in mid-field on a fumble, and set off for the adversary's goal; but the new players were not able to make much headway, and Deering, who had taken Pope's place, punted. The effort landed the ball on High School's thirty-seven, and her quarter ran it back eight more before he was stopped. Three tries at the line netted seven yards, and the visitor punted to Hop Kendrick on his eighteen. This time Hop hugged the ball hard and set off along the far side of the gridiron at a smart pace. Fortunately for him, one High School end overran. The other challenged, but missed his tackle. By that time a hasty interference had formed, and, guarded by Mason and Lightner, Hop reached his forty before misfortune overtook him. There a High School tackle crashed through the interference and nailed him hard.

But that twenty-yard sprint had brought new vim to the Blue's novices, and new confidence, and from their forty yards they began a fast, hard attack that placed High School with her back to the wall almost before she realized it. If the substitutes lacked the experience and brawn of the first-choice players, they at least had sand and speed. And they had a quarter-back who was earnest and grim and determined, and who, sensing that the opponent was weary, realized that speed, and a lot of it, was the one thing that could save the day. And so Hop proved his right to his nickname that afternoon. Hop he did, and so did his team. Signals were fairly shot into the air, and there was no longer any time between plays for High School to recover her breath. Twice, with plunges at the right of the visitor's line and runs outside her tackles, Hillman's made her distance and the pigskin rested on the thirty-six yards.

So far the Blue had attempted but three forward passes, of which only one had succeeded. Now, from position, Hop threw straight over the center, and somehow Lightner was there and pulled it down, although the enemy was clustered around him thick. That seven-yard gain was made ten when Deering was poked through the center, ten a little more, for the ball was down on High School's twenty-four-yard line. The game that had been proclaimed a practice event for the purpose of seasoning the substitutes against Saturday's contest had developed within the last half-hour into a battle to the death. Outside the gridiron the opposing factions hurled defiant cheers at each other and rooted as they had not rooted all the season. On the field the rivalry was even more intense, and black looks and hard knocks were the order.

High School, sparring for time, administered to a breathless right guard, and then drew into a bunch for a whispered conference, while Hillman's supporters hooted derisively. Deering gained three and Boessel two more. High School ran two substitutes on, and, after the next play, two more. An old-fashioned criss-cross sent Mason around his own right end for eight yards and planted the ball just short of the ten-yard line. Mason gave place to Beedle. A slide off tackle centered the pigskin and gained a scant yard. Deering struck center for a yard loss, and Lightner was caught off-side. The ball went back to the seventeen yards.

High School was playing desperately and her line had stiffened. Beedle gave way to Ned after that second down, and Ned had his instructions. The ball was in front of High School's goal, and from the seventeen yards a field goal was an easy proposition if the opponents could be held away from the kicker. Perhaps Hop Kendrick didn't realize why Ned had been sent in, or perhaps he thought better of his own judgment. Since by the rules Ned could not communicate the instructions from the coach until after the following play, he could only look his surprise when Hop failed to call him back to kicking position. Farley, captain in Stevenson's absence, seemed to be on the point of protesting, and even took a step toward the quarter-back; but he evidently reconsidered, for he returned to his position at the end of the line, and the starting signal followed.

The play was a fake attack on the right, with Boessel carrying the ball to the left inside of tackle, and it worked to perfection. High School, over-anxious, stormed to the defense of her threatened right side, and Boessel, with Ned hanging at his flank as far as the five-yard line, where the earth suddenly rose up and smote him, romped over the line for the last and deciding touch-down, while the Blue cohorts went fairly wild with delight.

On the side-line, Coach Mulford turned to Joe Stevenson. "What do you think of Kendrick?" he asked, smiling.

"I'd kiss him if I had him here," answered Joe, grinning joyously. "I call him one sweet little quarter, Coach!"

"Well, this was his day, all right," mused the other; "I hope he will show up as well Saturday. Now we'll see whether Turner can kick a goal. He's been doing some good work in practice, but he looks scared to death and will probably miss it by a mile."

And Ned *was* scared, too. He tried to steady his nerves by assuring himself that, whether he made it or missed it, the Blue had won the game, and that consequently a failure made little difference. But the silence of his schoolmates and the "booing" of the visiting rooters affected him badly. To Hop, holding the ball from the turf, it seemed that Ned would never have done pointing it. And so it seemed to the onlookers. Never was a kicker more deliberate. But at last Hop heard a faint "Down!" and drew his fingers from beneath the oval and waited an anxious moment. Then there was a clean, hard *thud*, and the quarter-back, watching its flight, saw the pigskin rise lazily, end over end, and go straight and high over the bar.

And he might have heard Ned's loud sigh of relief, had not the pounding of the charging enemy and the cries of the Hillman's horde drowned it.

Another kick-off and four plays ended the contest, and High School, after cheering half-heartedly, went off disgruntled and silent.

On his way to the field-house, Ned, trotting along with Hop, encountered Polly and Mae in the throng, and paused to speak. "Bully game, wasn't it?" he said. Then, seeing Mae's High School banner, he added: "High School put up a dandy fight, Mae."

"Indeed she did," agreed Mae. "I thought once she was going to win, too."

Polly was laughing. "Poor Mae didn't know which team she wanted to win," she explained. "When High School gained she waved her flag, and when Hillman's gained she waved it just the same. She was waving it all the time! That was a lovely goal you made, Nid."

"Thanks. I—well, I was so scared I didn't know whether to kick the ball or bite it! I'm mighty glad it went over, though." He nodded and hurried on in the wake of Hop, who, being a very earnest young gentleman and completely absorbed in the business of football, considered girls far outside his scheme of things.

Three quarters of an hour later, Laurie arose from his recumbent position on the window-seat of Number 16 East Hall, and delivered an ultimatum in quiet but forceful tones. "Ned," he said, "I saw that game from about the middle of the first quarter to the bitter end. Nothing escaped my eagle gaze. I can even tell you exactly how many times that High School umpire consulted his rules book when he thought no one was looking. I know how much dirt there was in Frank Brattle's left ear when they dragged him out. I know—"

"Well, what of it? What's your chief trouble?" growled Ned.

"Knowing all this and more, much more, Neddie, I refuse to listen any longer to your reminiscences. You've been through the game three times since you landed up here, and there's a limit to my endurance. And you've reached that limit, Neddie—you really have. I'm going down to George's, where I may hear something besides touch-downs and passes and goals. When you recover, Neddie, come on down."

"Oh, go to the dickens!" muttered Ned, as the door closed softly.

CHAPTER XVIII
BEFORE THE BATTLE

"The fellow who put these posts in," grunted Bob, as he heaved and tugged, "must have had more time than brains!"

It was Thursday afternoon. A hard frost, which had frozen the ground a half-inch deep, had counseled him to finish the work of wrecking the arbor. But three posts remained, and at one of these Bob, after having dug around it, and pried at it with a bar until patience was exhausted, was tugging lustily. Laurie, wiping the sweat of honest toil from his brow, cast aside the bar and gave a hand.

"Come on," he said hopefully. "One, two—three! Heave!"

"Heave!" muttered Bob.

But although the post, which had formed a corner of the arbor, gave from side to side, it refused to leave its nest. Panting, the boys drew off and observed it glumly.

"Guess we'll have to dig some more," said Bob.

"Wait a minute. Let me get a purchase on it with the bar."

Laurie seized that implement again and drove it into the softened earth beside the post. As the first drive didn't send it far enough, he pulled it out, and put all his strength into the next effort. This time he succeeded beyond all expectations. The bar slipped through his fingers and disappeared from sight!

"Well!" he gasped. "What do you know—"

"Where-where did it go to?" cried Bob, dumfounded.

"It went—it went to China, I guess! It just slipped right through my hands, and kept on slipping!" Laurie knelt and dug at the hole with his fingers.

"Find it?" asked Bob. "Try the shovel."

"No, I can't feel it. Hand it here." Laurie took the shovel and dug frantically. Then Bob dug. The result was that they enlarged and deepened the hole around the post, but the crowbar failed to materialize.

"I suppose," said Laurie, finally, dropping the shovel and tilting back his cap, "what happened was that I struck a sort of hole, and the bar went right down in. Maybe it was a rat-hole, Bob."

"I guess so. Anyway, it's gone, and we'll have to get a new one."

"Oh, I guess we'll find it when we get the post out. Let's try the old thing."

They did, and, after a moment of indecision, it came out most obligingly. But there was still no crowbar to be seen. Laurie shook his head, mystified. "That's the funniest thing I ever saw," he declared.

"It surely is! Look here; maybe there's an old well there."

"Then why didn't the post go down into it?"

"Because it's covered over with stones. The bar happened to slip into a—a crevice."

Laurie nodded dubiously. "That might be it," he agreed. "Or perhaps we've discovered a subterranean cavern!"

"Caverns always are subterranean, aren't they?"

"No; sometimes they're in the side of a hill."

"Then they're caves."

"A cave and a cavern are the same thing, you smart Aleck."

"All right; but even if a cavern is in a hill, it's underground, and subterranean means under—"

"Help! You win, Bob! Come on and get hold of this log and let's get it out of here." And, as they staggered with it across the garden to add it to the pile of posts and lumber already there, he continued: "There's one thing certain, Bob, and that's that you won't get me to play tennis on your court. I'd be afraid of sinking into the ground some fine day!"

"Maybe you'd find the crowbar then," said Bob. "Heave!"

Laurie "heaved," patted the brown loam from his hands, and surveyed the pile. "There's a lot of good stuff there," he pondered. "Some of it's sort of rotten, but there's enough to build something."

"What do you want to build?"

"I don't know. We could build a sort of covered seat, like the one in Polly's yard, where folks could rest and look on. Take about six of these posts and some of the strips, and some boards for the seat—"

"Who'd dig the post-holes?" inquired Bob, coldly.

"Oh, we could get a couple of the others to help. Honest, Bob, it would be a lot of fun. Maybe we couldn't do it before spring, though."

"I might leave the stuff here," said Bob. "Thomas could sort of pile it a little neater, you know. I love to carpenter. Sometime we'll draw a plan of it, Nod."

"Right-o! How about those other posts? No use trying to do anything with 'em to-day, is there?"

"No; we'll have to have another crowbar."

Laurie looked relieved. "Well, let's go over and see whether the Widow's got any of those little cakes with the chocolate on top," he suggested. "Hard work always makes a fellow hungry."

There was a rousing football meeting in the auditorium that evening, with speeches and music, songs and cheers; and the enthusiasm spilled over to the yard afterward, and threatened to become unruly until Dan Whipple mounted the steps of School Hall and spoke with all the authority of eighteen years and the senior class presidency. Whereupon someone suggested a cheer for the Doctor, and the joyous crowd thronged to the west end of the building and gave nine long "Hillman's," with a "Doctor Hillman" on the end. And then suddenly the lights flashed on on the porch, and there were the Doctor and Miss Tabitha, the former looking very much as if he had awakened very recently from a nap—which was, in fact, the case. But he was smiling as he stepped to the doorway and near-sightedly surveyed the throng.

"This—er—testimonial would appear to demand some sort of a response," he announced, as the applause that had greeted his appearance died away. "But I find myself singularly devoid of words, boys. Perhaps some of you recall the story of the visitor in Sunday-school who was unexpectedly called on by the superintendent to address the children. He hemmed and hawed and said, finally, that it gave him much pleasure to see so many smiling, happy faces. And he hoped they were all good little boys and girls and knew their lessons. And then his eloquence failed him, and after an unhappy interim he asked: 'And now, children, what shall I say?' And a little girl in the front row lisped: 'Pleathe, Mithter, thay "Amen" and thit down!'

"Perhaps I'd better say 'Amen' and sit down, too," he went on, when the laughter had ceased; "but before I do I'd like to assure you that I am 'rooting' just as hard as any of you for a victory the day after to-morrow. My duties will not allow me to see the team in action, as much as I'd like to, but I am kept well informed of its progress. I have my scouts at work constantly. Mr. Pennington reports to me on the work of the linemen; Mr. Barrett advises me each day as to the backs; Mr. Wells is my authority on—er—stratagem."

This amused his hearers intensely, since none of the three instructors mentioned had ever been known to attend a game or watch a practice.

"And," continued the principal, when he could, "I follow the newspaper reports of our enemy's progress. Of course, I don't believe all I read. If I did I'd be certain that only overwhelming disaster awaited us on Saturday. But there is one thing that troubles me. I read recently that the Farview center is a very large youth, weighing, if I am not mistaken, some one hundred and seventy pounds. While mere weight and brawn are not everything, I yet tremble to consider what may happen to the slight, atomic youth who will oppose him. Young gentlemen, I shudder when I dwell on that unequal meeting, that impending battle of David and Goliath!"

When the new burst of laughter had subsided, the doctor continued more soberly: "I wish the team all success, a notable victory. Or, if the gods of battle will it otherwise, I wish it the manly grace to accept defeat smilingly and undismayed. I am certain of one thing, boys, which is that, whether fortune favors the Dark Blue or the Maroon and White, the contest will be hard fought and clean, and bring honor alike to the victor and vanquished. You have my heartiest good wishes. And"—the doctor took the hand of Miss Tabitha, who had been standing a few steps behind him—"and the heartiest good wishes of another, who, while not a close follower of your sports, has a warm spot in her heart for each and every one of you, and who is as firmly convinced as I am of the invincibility of the Dark Blue!"

"Three cheers for Tab—for Miss Hillman!" cried a voice; and, at first a trifle ragged with laughter, the cheers rang forth heartily. Then came another cheer for the doctor and a rousing one for "Hillman's! *Hillman's!!* HILLMAN'S!!!" And the little throng, laughing and chattering, dispersed to the dormitories.

Friday saw but a light practice for the first team and a final appearance of the scrubs, who, cheered by the students, went through a few minutes of snappy signal work, and the waving sweaters and blankets dashed off to the field-house, their period of servitude at an end. For the first team there was a long blackboard drill in the gymnasium after supper, and Ned, who, somewhat to his surprise and very much to his gratification, had been retained on the squad, returned to Number 16 at nine o'clock in a rather bemused condition of mind. Kewpie, who accompanied him, tried to cheer him up.

"It'll be all right to-morrow, Nid," he declared. "I know how you feel. Fact is, I wouldn't know one signal from another if I got it this minute, and as for those sequences—" Words failed him. "But when you get on the field to-morrow it'll all come back to you. It—it's sort of psychological. A trick of memory and all that. You understand!"

"I don't see why he needs to worry, anyhow," observed Laurie, cruelly. "He won't get a show in to-morrow's game."

Ned looked hopeful for a moment, then relapsed into dejection as Kewpie answered: "I'd like to bet you he will, Nod. I'd like to bet you that he'll play a full period. You just watch Farview lay for Pope! Boy, they're going to make hard weather for that lad! They were after him last year, but they couldn't get him and he played right through. But I'd like to bet you that to-morrow they'll have him out of it before the last quarter."

"What do you mean?" asked Laurie, in surprise. "They don't play that sort of a game, do they?"

"What sort of a game?" responded Kewpie. "They play hard, that's the way they play! And every time they tackle Pope, they'll tackle him so he'll know it. And every time he hits the line, there'll be one of those red-legs waiting for him. Oh, they don't play dirty, if you mean that; but they don't let any chances slip, believe me!"

"It sounds sort of off color to me, though," Laurie objected. "How are you going to put a fellow out of the game if you don't slug or do something like that?"

Kewpie smiled knowingly. "My son," he said, "if I start after you and run you around the dormitory about twenty times—"

Ned, in spite of his down-heartedness, snickered at the picture evolved, and Kewpie grinned.

"Well, suppose some one else did, then. Anyhow, after he'd done it about a couple of dozen times, you'd be all in, wouldn't you? He wouldn't have to kick you or knock you down or anything, would he? Well, that's what I mean. That's the way they'll go after Pope. They'll tire him out. You understand. And every time they tackle him, they'll tackle him good and hard. Well, suppose Pope does go out, and there's a chance for a field goal, as there's likely to be. Who will Pinky put in? Why, Nid, of course! Who else is there? Brattle can't kick one goal in six. No more can Deering. What do you think Mulford's been nursing Nid all the season for?"

"Next year?" said Laurie, questioningly.

"Sure—and this year, too. You watch and see. I'd like to bet you that Nid'll have a goal to kick to-morrow—yes, and that he'll kick it, too!"

"Don't!" groaned Ned. "I never could do it!"

"Well," laughed Laurie, "I don't bet for money, Kewpie, but I tell you what I'll do. If Ned kicks a goal to-morrow, I'll take you over to the Widow's, and I'll buy you all the cream-puffs you can eat at one sitting!"

"It's a go!" cried Kewpie. "And if he doesn't, I'll do it to you!"

"Of course," explained Laurie, in recognition of his brother's look of pained inquiry, "I'm not making the offer because I think Ned can't do it, or because I don't want him to play. You bet I do! It's because I do want him to, Kewpie. You see, I usually lose bets!"

"All right, you crazy galoot. I've got to beat it. Pinky made us swear by the Great Horn Spoon to be in bed by ten. Good night. Don't let the signal stuff worry you, Nid. It'll come out all right to-morrow. You understand. Night!"

When the door had closed, Laurie laughed and turned to Ned. "He's a good old scout, isn't he? I say, what's the matter with you, Ned? You look like the end of a hard winter! Cheer up! It may not be true!"

But Ned shook his head, although he tried to smile unconcernedly. "It'll happen just the way he told, Laurie," he said, sadly. "I just know it will! They'll get Pope out of the way, and there'll be a field goal wanted, just as there was Wednesday, and Mulford will send me in!"

"Well, what of it? You'd like that, wouldn't you?"

"I—I'm scared!"

"Oh, piffle, Neddie! You've got nerves, that's all. The night before the battle, you know, and all that! In the morning you'll be as right as rain. Get your clothes off and tumble in. Want me to read a story to you? There's a corker in the 'Post' this week."

"No, thanks; I guess not. I'd better go to sleep."

But, although Ned, stifling a desire to sit up and read the corking story himself, put the light out at ten minutes before ten, he lay awake until after midnight and suffered as blue a case of funk as any boy ever did. And when, at length, sleep came, it was filled with visions in which he stood in the center of a vast arena, the object of countless eyes, and tried over and over, and never with success, to kick a perfectly gigantic leather ball over a cross-bar that was higher than the Masonic Temple at home!

The truth is that Ned was over-trained and stale. And the further truth is that when he awoke to as sweet a November morning as ever peered down from a cloudless sky through golden sunlight, he felt, as he phrased it to himself, like a sock that had just come through the wringer!

CHAPTER XIX
NED IS MISSING

Ned ate almost no breakfast, and Laurie noted the fact, but, after a glance at his brother's face, said nothing. After all, he reflected, there were probably others of the squad who were displaying no more appetite this morning. Afterward, on the way to School Hall for their only recitation of the day, he asked off-handedly: "How are you feeling, Neddie?"

Ned didn't answer at once. When he did, he only replied laconically: "Rotten!"

"How do you mean, rotten?" Laurie disguised anxiety under flippancy. "Tummy out of whack? Or is it a case of ingrowing signals?"

"I don't know what the trouble is," answered Ned seriously. "I feel perfectly punk. And I—I'm scared, Laurie. I'd give a million dollars if I didn't have to go to the field this afternoon. I wish to goodness I could duck somehow. Say, feel my forehead. Isn't it hot?"

Laurie felt, and shook his head. "Cool as a cucumber, you old fakir. Buck up, Neddie! You'll feel better after a while. Did you sleep all right?"

"I guess so," replied the other dispiritedly. "I dreamed a lot. Dreamed I was kicking goals over a bar as high as a mountain. And the ball was as big as a hogshead. And there were about a million folks watching me, and Mr. Cornish was beating a bass-drum."

Laurie laughed. "Some dream, Neddie! Tell you what. After we get out of here, we'll take a nice, long hike. Mulford wants the players to stay outdoors, doesn't he? Didn't you tell me he said you were to walk or something?"

Ned nodded. "I'm too tired to walk, though, Laurie. Guess I'll get a book and go over to the park. Or go down and jump in the river!"

"Fine idea!" scoffed Laurie. "What have you got against the river? It never did anything to you, did it?"

Ned, however, refused to smile. "You don't need to come along," he said. "I—I guess I'd rather be alone, Laurie."

"You will be, if you're going to jump in the river, partner! The water's a heap too cold to appeal to me. Well, cheer up. See you when we come out."

There was a holiday feeling in the air this morning that didn't promise well for recitations, and Mr. Brock's chemistry class was a sore trial to that gentleman. Yet, although he frowned often and sighed many despairing sighs, he made allowance for the prevailing mood of restlessness and exhibited unusual patience. And finally it was over and the class trooped out.

"You stay here," said Laurie, "and I'll run over and get a couple of books from the room. What do you want?"

"I don't care—anything," answered Ned, listlessly.

When Laurie went off, Ned seated himself on a step and gazed forlornly around him. Groups of boys stood on the walks in animated conversation. Near at hand, a half-dozen juniors were discussing the game avidly, drawing comforting conclusions from a comparison of the season's performances of Hillman's and Farview. Suddenly the prospect of sitting on a park bench with Laurie became utterly distasteful to Ned, and, with a hurried glance in the direction of East Hall, he arose and made his way along the drive and into Summit Street. There he turned to the left and walked quickly to the corner. At Washington Street another look behind showed that he had made his escape, and he heaved a sigh of relief and went on past the library and into Cumber Street, heading unconsciously toward the open country eastward of town.

When Laurie returned to School Hall with a book for Ned and a magazine for himself, he sat down and waited a few minutes, supposing that Ned would be back. When he didn't come, Laurie went over to School Park, thinking that he had perhaps grown tired of waiting in the yard. But no Ned was to be seen, and, puzzled but untroubled, Laurie dawdled into Pine Street. The white-and-red sign above the Widow Deane's little store shone bravely in the sunlight. For an hour Laurie enjoyed the society of Polly and Antoinette in the sunny garden, where, against the board fence, a clump of hardy chrysanthemums made a cheery showing of yellow and lavender. Antoinette had retired to winter quarters, which means that a gunny-sack and a length of old red carpet had been draped over her box. But just now the drapery was lifted, and Antoinette was doing great things to a very large cabbage-leaf. Towser had established himself in the sunshine atop the porch roof and gazed down benignly at the pair below.

Laurie and Polly talked, of course, about the game. He and George were again to act as escorts to the two girls, a fact that had eaten a large hole in Laurie's remaining allowance. About ten o'clock he took himself away, reminding Polly to be ready at half-past one, since it took a good ten minutes to walk to the field, and because, wisely, he realized that to Polly "half-past one" would mean a quarter or two. Climbing the fence into Bob's yard, he discovered that young man with a new crowbar about to begin an attack on the remaining posts of the arbor. So he removed his sweater, moistened his hands in the time-honored and only efficacious manner, and joined the assault. After the posts were added to the pile beside the fence, the two boys went indoors and refreshed the inner man with piping-hot ginger cookies. Thus it was that it was nearly noon when Laurie got back to Number 16, to find, to his uneasiness, that Ned was not there. Nor, as far as any evidences showed, had he been there since before breakfast.

Laurie threw himself on the window-seat and tried to apply himself to the magazine that he had carried all morning. But he began to be really worried about Ned. He didn't understand where he could be. Even if he had gone off by himself, mooning along the roads, which was what Laurie suspected he had done, he should have been home before this, for, as Laurie knew, the players were to go to lunch at twelve. Presently he dropped the magazine and strode across the corridor to Number 15. Kewpie was not in, but Hop was there—a more than ordinarily serious-faced Hop, who replied to Laurie's inquiry in an absent-minded manner suggesting that some one had placed him in a trance and gone away without awakening him. Hop hadn't seen Nid all morning. Kewpie had just gone over to West Hall. He hoped there wouldn't be any wind this afternoon. Farview had a punter that could do fifty yards easily, and a wind would lengthen his kicks frightfully. Did Nod think those clouds meant wind?

Laurie withdrew without venturing an opinion in the matter. Football, he reflected, was a far more dangerous pastime than folks generally realized, when it could affect a fellow's brains like that! Downstairs, he searched the little group about the dining-hall door, and finally made inquiry of Dave Murray. Dave was worried and excited and a bit short-tempered.

"Nid Turner? No, I haven't seen him. He'll be here pretty quick, though. We eat at twelve."

He left Laurie, to push his way toward the entrance to accost Mr. Mulford, who was coming in; and Laurie went out and sat down on the step and watched. Kewpie came striding across from West Hall, smiling and evidently very fit. But when Laurie questioned him the smile faded.

"Nid? No, I haven't set eyes on him. Isn't he here? Are you sure? Say, you don't suppose the silly guy has bolted? He was in mean shape last night, Nod. But he wouldn't do that! He's no quitter. He'll be here in a minute or two."

"Suppose—suppose he isn't?" asked Laurie, anxiously. "Would it matter much?"

"Matter?" Kewpie shrugged, one eye on the dining-hall door, through which his team-mates were beginning to pass. "It wouldn't matter to the game, I guess. I was only trying to cheer him up last night. You understand. It isn't likely Pinky will use him. But it would be a bad thing for him, Nod. It would be an awful black eye, in fact, if he cut the game. Guess Pinky would just about can him for all time! I say, I've got to hustle in there. Why don't you have a look around for him? Maybe he's in the library, or over in West, or—or somewhere. See you later, Nod!"

Kewpie disappeared into the dining-hall, and a moment later the door was closed. Laurie acted on Kewpie's suggestion, and made a thorough search of School Hall and the other dormitory, and even poked his head into the gymnasium, where only an empty floor met his gaze. After that there seemed nothing to do but wait. Ned had already missed his lunch, for the fellows were coming out into the corridor when Laurie returned to East Hall. Murray nailed him as he tried to pass unnoticed to the stairs.

"Say, Nod, where's that brother of yours?" he demanded indignantly. "Didn't he know that lunch was at twelve? Where is he, anyway?"

"I don't know, Dave," Laurie answered, miserably. "He went for a walk this morning, and I haven't seen him since. I guess he went too far and couldn't get back in time. I've been looking all over for him."

"That's fine!" said the manager, bitterly. "Mulford asked for him, and I said I'd look him up. You'd better find him mighty quick, Nod. Tell him to get something to eat somewhere and be at the gym not later than one. There's a floor drill then. I'll make it all right with Mulford, somehow. But there'll be the dickens and all to pay if he doesn't show up!"

Hoping against hope, Laurie hurried up to the room. But there was no Ned. One o'clock came and passed. Time and again Laurie went to the gate and looked up and down the street, but without result. Ned had disappeared utterly, it seemed, and the unwelcome conclusion grew in Laurie's mind that Ned had shown the white feather and had deliberately absented himself. Laurie didn't like to think that, and there were moments when he couldn't. But here it was nearly half-past one, and Ned hadn't come, and facts are facts! It looked, he thought sadly, like a bad day for the honor of the Turners!

At half-past one he found George Watson in his room, and handed over one of his tickets. "I can't go to the field with you," he said, "but I'll find you over there. Try to keep a seat for me, will you?"

"What's the big idea?" asked George, blankly. "Why can't you go with us? That's a fine game to play!"

"I'll tell you later. I—I've got something to do. Be a good fellow, George, won't you? And tell Polly how it is, will you?"

"How the dickens can I tell Polly how it is when I don't know how it is myself?" asked George, indignantly. "Oh, all right! But you want to get there pretty quick, Nod. It's hard to hold seats when there aren't enough of them in the first place. There's a regular mob going out there already!"

Disconsolately Laurie hurried out and stationed himself at the dormitory entrance. Presently the players emerged from the gymnasium in their togs and passed through the little gate to Washington Street. Laurie watched them file past, hoping hard that Ned would be among them. But, although all the rest were there, twenty-one in all, there was no Ned.

From Washington Street and Summit Street came a steady tramping of feet, accompanied by a swishing sound as the pedestrians brushed through the fallen leaves. Occasionally an automobile went by with a warning honk of its horn at the corner. Looking over the withered hedge, Laurie could see the colors of Hillman's and Farview marching past, banners of dark blue bearing the white Old English H, maroon-and-white flags adorned with the letters "F. A." Laughter and the merry, excited chatter of many voices came to him. The yard was empty, except for a boy hurrying down the steps of West Hall, and he too quickly disappeared through the gate.

Presently Laurie looked at his watch. The time was eighteen minutes to two. He left East Hall and turned toward the gymnasium. Out of the shelter of the dormitory a little breeze fanned his face, and he remembered Hop Kendrick's dread of a wind that would put more power into the toe of the Farview punter. It might be, he reflected, that Hop was due for disappointment; but the matter didn't seem very important to him. The locker-room in the gymnasium was empty. Over the benches lay the discarded underclothing of the players, and sometimes the outer clothing as well, suggesting that excitement on this occasion had prevailed over orderliness. Laurie made his way to Ned's locker. It was closed, and behind the unfastened door hung his togs.

CHAPTER XX
FOR THE HONOR OF THE TURNERS

Walking felt good to Ned that morning. The air, brisk in spite of the sunshine and the day's stillness, cleared his head of the queer cloudiness that had been there since awakening, and, turning into the country road that led eastward toward the higher hills, he strode along briskly. He had, he reflected, played rather a low-down trick on Laurie; but that could be explained later, and Laurie wouldn't mind when he understood. When he had gone the better part of a mile into the country, and the road had begun to steepen perceptibly, the sound of a motor behind warned him to one side. But, instead of passing in a cloud of dust, the automobile slowed down as it reached the pedestrian, and the driver, a genial-looking man of middle age, hailed.

"Going my way?" he asked. "Get in if you like."

Ned hesitated, and then climbed in beside the solitary occupant of the car. The prospect of speeding through the sunlit morning world appealed to him, and he thanked the driver and snuggled into the other corner of the front seat.

"That's all right, my boy," answered the man, genially. "Glad to have company. How far are you going?"

"Just—just up the road a ways," replied Ned, vaguely. "I was out for a walk, only this seemed better."

"Well, it's quicker, though it doesn't give you quite so much exercise," was the response. "You sing out when you've had enough. Maybe you can get a lift going back, if you're not in too much of a hurry. Still, there isn't much travel on this road. Most folks go around by Little Windsor. It's longer, but the road's a sight better. I go this way because I can do it quicker. There are some fierce bumps, though. Yell if you drop out!"

The car was a heavy one with good springs, and as long as Ned remained in it the bad bumps didn't materialize. His companion evidently liked to talk, and Ned learned a good deal about him and his business, without, however, finding it very interesting. The man asked few questions, and so Ned merely supplied the information that he was from Hillman's School and that he liked to walk and that he had all the morning to get back in. The car kept up an even, effortless speed of twenty-seven or -eight miles an hour, and it was finding himself booming up the straight grade over Candle Mountain that brought Ned to a sudden realization that if he meant to get back to school by twelve o'clock without undue effort he had best part company with his chatty acquaintance. So, at the summit of the hill, he said good-by, repeated his thanks, and got out.

"Guess you're about six miles from Orstead," said the man. "It won't take you long to get back there, though, if you find a lift. Don't hesitate to stop any one you see; they'll be glad to take you in. Good-by!"

The gray automobile went on and was speedily dropping from sight beyond the nearly leafless forest. Ned watched it disappear, and then set his face toward home. The ride had certainly done him good, he told himself. The prospect of being called on to kick a dozen goals wouldn't have dismayed him a mite at that moment. In fact, he suddenly realized that he was going to be horribly disappointed if the chance to attempt at least one goal from the field did not come to him, and he wondered why he had felt so craven last night.

After a mile or so a small, dust-covered car overhauled him and went by without a challenge from him. It was still only ten o'clock, and he had two hours yet, and he had no intention of begging a ride. Taken leisurely, the remaining miles would be covered without weariness and in plenty of time. When he had accomplished, as he reckoned, about half the distance to Orstead, his watch said seventeen minutes to eleven. The forenoon had grown appreciably warmer, and so had Ned. Beside the road was a little knoll carpeted with ashy-brown beech-leaves. Only a stone wall, bordered with blackberry briars, intervened.

Ned climbed across the wall and seated himself on the slope of the knoll. The land descended gently before him toward the river and the town, but neither was in sight. Presently, removing his cap, he stretched himself on his back and linked his fingers under his head. And presently, because the blue, sunlit, almost cloudless sky was too dazzling to gaze at long, he closed his eyes. And as he did so a strange, delicious languor descended upon him. He sighed luxuriously and stretched his legs into a more comfortable position. It was odd that he should feel sleepy at this time of day, he thought, and it wouldn't do to stay here too long. He wished, though, that he didn't have to get anywhere at any especial time. It would be great to just lie here like this and feel the sun on his face and—

At about that moment he stopped thinking at all and went sound asleep.

When he awoke he was in shadow, for the sun had traveled around and past the elbow of a near-by old and knotted oak whose brown-pink leaves still clung to the twisted branches. Ned looked around him in puzzlement, and it was a long moment before he could account for his surroundings. When he had, he sat up very quickly and gave a startled look at his watch. The thing was crazy! It said twenty-one minutes past two! Of course it couldn't be that late, he told himself indignantly. But even as he said it he was oppressed by a conviction that it was. And a look at the sun removed any lingering doubt!

He sprang to his feet, seized his cap, and stumbled across the wall, and, again on the road, set out at a run toward home. But after a moment he slowed up. "Was there any use in hurrying now? The game was already in progress— had been going on for twenty minutes. The first quarter was probably nearly over. What would they say to him, the fellows and Coach Mulford and— Laurie? Somehow, what Laurie would think appeared far more important than what any of the others might. He would have such a poor excuse, he reflected ruefully! Went for a walk, and fell asleep by the road! Gee, he couldn't tell them that! He might tell Laurie; but the others—"

He was jogging on as he thought things over. Even if he ran all the way, and he couldn't do that, of course, he wouldn't get to school before three. And then he would have to change into his togs and reach the field. And by that time the second half would have started. Wouldn't it be far better to remain away altogether? He might easily reach his room unseen, and then, when Laurie returned, he could pretend illness. He might not fool Laurie; but the others, Coach Mulford and Dave Murray and the fellows, would have to believe him.

If a fellow was ill, he couldn't be expected to play football. He even got as far as wondering what particular and peculiar malady he could assume, when he put the idea aside.

"No use lying about it," he muttered. "Got to face the music, Ned! It was your own fault. Maybe Mulford will let me down easy. I wouldn't like to queer myself for next year. Gee, though, what'll the school think?" And Ned groaned aloud.

While he had slept, five vehicles had passed him, and as many persons had seen him lying there asleep in the sun and idly conjectured about him. But now, when he needed help to conquer the interminable three miles that stretched between him and the town, and although he constantly turned his head to gaze hopefully back along the dusty road, not a conveyance appeared. Before long, since he had unwisely started at too great a speed, he was forced to sit down on a rock and rest. He was very nearly out of breath and the perspiration was trickling down beneath his cloth cap. A light breeze had sprung up since he had dropped asleep, and it felt very grateful as it caressed his damp hair and flushed face.

Perhaps those three miles were nearer four, because when, tired, dusty, and heart-sick, he descried the tower of the Congregational church above the leafless elms and maples of the village, the gilded hands pointed to twelve minutes past three. Even had he arrived in time, he reflected miserably, he would never have been able to serve his team-mates and his school, for he was scarcely able to drag one foot behind the other as he finally turned into the yard.

The place appeared deserted, grounds and buildings alike, as Ned unhesitatingly made his way across to the gymnasium. He had long since decided on his course of action. No matter whether he had failed his coach and his schoolmates, his duty was still plain. As late as it was, he would get into his togs and report at the field. But when, in the empty locker-room, he paused before where his football togs should have been, he found only empty hooks. The locker, save for towels, was empty!

At first he accepted the fact as conclusive evidence of his disgrace—thought that coach or manager or an infuriated student body had removed his clothes as a signal of degradation! Then the unlikelihood of the conclusion came, and he wondered whether they had really been there. But of course they had! He remembered perfectly hanging them up, as usual, yesterday afternoon. Perhaps some one had borrowed them, then. The locker had been unfastened, probably, for half the time he forgot to turn the key in it. Wondering, he made his way out of the building, undecided now what to do. But as he reached the corner a burst of cheers floated to him from the play-field. His head came up. It was still his duty to report, togs or no togs! Resolutely he set out on Summit Street, the sounds of battle momentarily growing nearer as he limped along.

By the entrances many automobiles and some carriages lined the road. Above the stand the backs of the spectators in the top row of seats looked strangely agitated, and blue flags waved and snapped. A fainter cheer came to him, the slogan of Farview, from the farther side of the field. He heard the piping of signals, and a dull thud of leather against leather, then cries and a whistle shrilling; and then a great and triumphant burst of cheering from the Blue side.

He hurried his steps, leaped the low fence beside the road, and came to a group of spectators standing at the nearer end of the long, low grand stand. He could see the gridiron now, and the battling teams in mid-field. And the scoreboard at the farther end! And, seeing that, his heart sank. "Hillman's 7—Visitors 9" was the story! He tugged the sleeve of a man beside him, a youngish man in a chauffeur's livery.

"What period is it?" he asked.

"Fourth," was the answer. The man turned a good-natured look on the boy's anxious face.

"Been going about four minutes. You just get here?"

Ned nodded. "How did they get their nine?" he asked.

"Farview? Worked a forward pass in the second quarter for about thirty yards, and smashed over for a touch-down. They failed at goal, though. That made 'em six, and they got three more in the last quarter. Hillman's fumbled about on their thirty, and that bandy-legged full-back of Farview's kicked a corking goal from field. Gee—say, it was some kick!"

"Placement or drop?"

"Drop. Almost forty yards, I guess. There they go again!" The chauffeur tiptoed to see over a neighbor's head. Ned, past his shoulder, had an uncertain glimpse of the Maroon and White breaking through the Blue's left side. When the down was signaled, he spoke again.

"How did Hillman's score?" he asked.

"Huh? Oh, she got started right off at the beginning of the game and just ate those red-legs up. Rushed the ball from the middle of the field, five and six yards at a whack, and landed it on the other fellow's door-sill. Farview sort of pulled together then and made a fight; but that big chap, Pope, the full-back, smashed through finally, right square between the posts. After that he kicked the goal. Guess the red-legs had stage-fright then, but they got over it, and our fellows haven't had a chance to score since. Pope had to lay off last quarter. They played him to a standstill. Mason's mighty good, but he can't make the gains Pope did. First down again! Say, they aren't doing a thing but eating us up!"

Ned wormed himself to the front of the group, and came to anchor at the side of a tall policeman, close to the rope that stretched from the end of the stand well past the zone line. By craning his neck he could look down the length of the field. White-sweatered, armed with big blue megaphones, Brewster and Whipple and two others, cheer leaders, were working mightily, although the resulting cheers sounded weak where Ned stood. The teams were coming down the field slowly but surely, the Blue contesting every yard, but yielding after every play. The lines faced each other close to the thirty now. Across the gridiron, Farview's pæans were joyful and confident, and the maroon-and-white flags gyrated in air. Well back toward his threatened goal, Hop Kendrick, white-faced and anxious, called hoarse encouragement. Ned clenched his hands and hoped and feared.

A line attack turned into an unexpected forward pass, and a tall Farview end came streaking down just inside the boundary. Hop was after him like a shot; but Deering, who had taken Pope's place, ran him out at the fifteen-yard line. The Maroon and White went wild with joy. The teams trooped in on the heels of the diminutive referee, and the ball was down just inside Hillman's fifteen. Ned looked the Blue team over. Save for Corson and White, the line was made up of first-string men, but the back field was, with the single exception of Mason, all substitutes: Kendrick, Boessel, and Deering.

A plunge straight at the center gave Farview two more precious yards, Kewpie, apparently pretty well played out, yielding before the desperate attack. Three more yards were gained between Emerson and Stevenson on the left. Third down now, and five to go! Evidently Farview was determined on a touch-down, for on the nine yards, with an excellent chance for a field goal, she elected to rush again. But this time the Blue's center held, and the Farview left half, when friend and foe was pulled from above him, held the pigskin scarcely a foot in advance of its former position. It was Hillman's turn to cheer, and cheer she did. Ned added a wild shout of triumph to the din about him.

Fourth down, and still five yards to gain! Now Farview must either kick or try a forward, and realizing this the Blue's secondary defense dropped back and out. A Farview substitute came speeding on, a new left tackle. Then, amid a sudden hush, the quarter sang his signals: "Kick formation! 73—61—29—" The big full-back stretched his arms out. "12—17—9!" Back sped the ball, straight and breast-high. The Blue line plunged gallantly. The stand became a pandemonium. The full-back swung a long right leg, but the ball didn't drop from his hands. Two steps to the left, and he was poising it for a forward pass! Then he threw, well over the up-stretched hands of a Hillman's player who had broken through, and to the left. A Maroon and White end awaited the ball, for the instant all alone on the Blue's goal-line. Ned, seeing, groaned dismally. Then from somewhere a pair of blue-clad arms flashed into sight, a slim body leaped high, and from the Hillman's side of the field came a veritable thunder of relief and exultation. For the blue arms had the ball, and the blue player was dodging and worming toward the farther side-line! Captain Stevenson it was who cleared the path for him at the last moment, bowling over a Farview player whose arms were already stretched to grapple, and, in a shorter time than the telling takes, Hop Kendrick was racing toward the distant goal!

Afterward Ned realized that during the ensuing ten or twelve seconds he had tried desperately to shin up the tall policeman; but at the time he had not known it, nor, or so it appeared, had the policeman, for the latter was shouting his lungs out! Past the middle of the field sped Hop, running as fleetly as a hare, and behind him pounded a solitary Farview end. These two left the rest of the field farther and farther back at every stride. For a moment it seemed that Hop would win that desperate race; but at last, near the thirty-five yards, he faltered, and the gap between him and his pursuer closed to a matter of three or four strides, and after that it was only a question of how close to the goal the Blue runner would get before he was overtaken and dragged down. The end came between the fifteen- and twenty-yard streaks.

Then, no more than a stride behind, the Farview player sprang. His arms wrapped themselves around Hop's knees, and the runner crashed to earth.

For a long minute the babel of shouting continued, for that eighty-yard sprint had changed the complexion of the game in a handful of seconds. Hillman's was no longer the besieged, fighting in her last trench to stave off defeat, but stood now on the threshold of victory, herself the besieger!

Farview called for time. Two substitutes came in to strengthen her line. Hop, evidently no worse for his effort, was on his feet again, thumping his players on the backs, imploring, entreating, and confident. On the seventeen yards lay the brown oval, almost in front of the right-hand goal-post. A field goal would put the home team one point to the good, and, with only a few minutes left to play, win the game almost beyond a doubt, and none on the Blue's side of the field doubted that a try at goal would follow. Even when the first play came from ordinary formation and Deering smashed into the left of Farview's line for a scant yard, the audience was not fooled. Of course, it was wise to gain what ground they might with three downs to waste, for there was always the chance that a runner might get free and that luck would bring a touch-down instead.

Yet again Hop signaled a line attack. This time it was Mason who carried the ball, and he squirmed through for two yards outside left tackle, edging the pigskin nearer the center of the goal. Then came a shout that started near the Blue team's bench and traveled right along the stand. A slight youngster was pulling off his sweater in front of the bench, a boy with red-brown hair and a pale, set face. Then he had covered the red-brown hair with a leather helmet and was trotting into the field with upraised hand.

Ned stared and stared. Then he closed his eyes for an instant, opened them, and stared again. After that he pinched himself hard to make certain that he was awake and not still dreaming on the knoll beside the road. The substitute was speaking to the referee now, and Deering was walking away from the group in the direction of the bench. The cheering began, the leaders waving their arms in unison along the length of the Hillman's stand:

"'Rah, 'rah, 'rah! 'Rah, 'rah, 'rah! 'Rah, 'rah, 'rah! Deering!"

And then again, a second later: "'Rah, 'rah, 'rah! 'Rah, 'rah, 'rah! 'Rah, 'rah, 'rah! Turner!"

Ned turned imploringly to the tall policeman. "What—who was that last fellow they cheered?" he faltered.

The policeman looked down impatiently.

"Turner. Guess he's going to kick a goal for 'em."

CHAPTER XXI
THE UNDERSTUDY

"*Block that kick! Block that kick! Block that kick!*" chanted Farview imploringly, from across the trampled field.

Yet above the hoarse entreaty came Hop Kendrick's confident voice: "All right, Hillman's! Make it go! Here's where we win it! Kick formation! Turner back!" And then: "25—78—26—194! 12—31—9—"

But it was Hop himself who dashed straight forward and squirmed ahead over one white line before the whistle blew.

"Fourth down!" called the referee. "About four and a half!"

"Come on!" cried Hop. "Make it go this time! Hard, fellows, hard! We've got 'em going!" He threw an arm over the shoulder of the new substitute. Those near by saw the latter shake his head, saw Hop draw back and stare as if aghast at the insubordination. Farview protested to the referee against the delay, and the latter called warningly. Hop nodded, and raised his voice again:

"Kick formation! Turner back!"

Then he walked back to where the substitute stood and dropped to his knees.

"Place-kick!" grunted a man at Ned's elbow. "Can't miss it from there if the line holds!"

Ned, in a perfect agony of suspense, waited. Hop was calling his signals. There was a pause. Then: "16—32—7—"

Back came the ball on a long pass from Kewpie. It was high, but Hop got it, pulled it down, and pointed it. Ned saw the kicker step forward. Then he closed his eyes.

There was a wild outburst from all around him, and he opened them again. The ball was not in sight, but a frantic little man in a gray sweater was waving his arms like a semaphore behind the farther goal. Along the space between stand and side-line a quartette of youths leaped crazily, flourishing great blue megaphones or throwing them in air. Above the stand blue banners waved and caps tossed about. On the scoreboard at the far end of the field the legend read: "Hillman's 10—Visitors 9."

A moment later, a boy with a wide grin on his tired face and nerves that were still jangling made his way along Summit Street in the direction of school. Behind him the cheers and shouts still broke forth at intervals, for there yet remained some three minutes of playing time. Once, in the sudden stillness between cheers, he heard plainly the hollow thump of a punted ball. More shouts then, indeterminate, dying away suddenly. The boy walked quickly, for he had a reason for wanting to gain the security of his room before the crowd flowed back from the field. At last, at the school gate, he paused and looked back and listened. From the distant scene of battle came a faint surge of sound that rose and fell and rose again and went on unceasingly as long as he could hear.

Back in Number 16, Ned threw his cap aside and dropped into the nearest chair. There was much that he understood, yet much more that was still a mystery to him. One thing, however, he dared hope, and that was that the disgrace of having failed his fellows had passed him miraculously by! As to the rest, he pondered and speculated vainly. He felt horribly limp and weary while he waited for Laurie to come. And after a while he heard cheering, and arose and went to a window. There could no longer be any doubt as to the final outcome of the game. Between the sidewalk throngs, dancing from side to side of the street with linked arms, came Hillman's, triumphant!

"Turner. Guess he's going to kick a goal for 'em."

And here and there, borne on the shoulders of joyous comrades, bobbed a captured player. There were more than a dozen of them, some taking the proceeding philosophically, others squirming and fighting for freedom. Now and then one succeeded in getting free, but recapture was invariably his fate. At least, this was true with a single exception while Ned watched. The exception was a boy with red-brown hair, who, having managed to slip from his enthusiastic friends, dashed through the throng on the sidewalk, leaped a fence, cut across a corner, and presently sped through the gate on Washington Street, pursuit defeated. A minute later, flushed and breathless, he flung open the door of Number 16.

At sight of Ned, Laurie's expression of joyous satisfaction faded. He halted inside the door and closed it slowly behind him. At last, "Hello," he said, listlessly.

"Hello," answered Ned. Then there was a long silence. Outside, in front of the gymnasium, they were cheering the victorious team, player by player. At last, "We won, didn't we?" asked Ned.

Laurie nodded as if the thing were a matter of total indifference. He still wore football togs, and he frowningly viewed a great hole in one blue stocking as he seated himself on his bed.

"Well," he said, finally, "what happened to you?"

Ned told him, at first haltingly, and then with more assurance as he saw the look of relief creep into Laurie's face. As he ended his story, Laurie's countenance expressed only a great and joyous amusement.

"Neddie," he chuckled, "you'll be the death of me yet! You came pretty near to it to-day, too, partner!" He sobered as his thoughts went back to a moment some fifteen minutes before, and he shook his head. "Partner, this thing of understudying a football hero is mighty wearing. I'm through for all time. After this, Ned, you'll have to provide your own substitute! I'm done!"

"How—why—how did you happen to think of it?" asked Ned, rather humbly. "Weren't you—scared?"

"Scared? Have a heart! I was frightened to death every minute I sat on the bench. And then, when Mulford yelped at me, I—well, I simply passed away altogether! I'm at least ten years older than I was this morning, Neddie, and I'll bet I've got gray hairs all over my poor old head. You see, Murray as much as said that it was all day with you if you didn't show up. Kewpie was a bit down-hearted about it, too. I waited around until half-past one or after, thinking every moment that you'd turn up—hoping you would, anyhow; although, to be right honest, Neddie, I had a sort of hunch, after the way you acted and talked, that maybe you'd gone off on purpose. Anyhow, about one o'clock I got to thinking, and the more I thought the more I got into the notion that something had to be done if the honor of the Turners was to be—be upheld. And the only thing I could think of was putting on your togs and bluffing it through. Kewpie owned up that he'd been talking rot last night—that he didn't really think you'd be called on to-day. And I decided to take a chance. Of course, if I'd known what was going to happen I guess I wouldn't have had the courage; but I didn't know. I thought all I'd have to do was sit on the bench and watch.

"So I went over to the gym and got your togs on, and streaked out to the field, I guess I looked as much like you as you do, for none of the fellows knew that I wasn't you. I was careful not to talk much. Mr. Mulford gave me thunder, and so did Murray, and Joe Stevenson looked pretty black. I just said I was sorry, and there wasn't much time to explain, anyway, because the game was starting about the time I got there. Once, in the third period, when Slavin was hurt, Mulford looked along the bench and stopped when he got to me, and I thought my time had come. But I guess he wanted to punish me for being late. Anyway, Boessel got the job. When the blow did fall, Neddie, I was sick clean through. My tummy sort of folded up and my spine was about as stiff as—as a drink of water! I wanted to run, or crawl under the bench or something. 'You've pleased yourself so far to-day, Turner,' said Mulford. 'Now suppose you do something for the school. Kendrick will call for a kick. You see that it gets over, or I'll have something to say to you later. Remember this, though: not a word to any one but the referee until after the next play. Now get out there and *win this game!*'

"Nice thing to say to a chap who'd never kicked a football in his life except around the street! But, gee, Neddie, what could I do? I'd started the thing, and I had to see it through. Of course I thought that maybe I'd ought to fess up that I wasn't me—or, rather, you—and let some one else kick. But I knew there wasn't any one else they could depend on, and I decided that if some one had to miss the goal, it might as well be me—or you. Besides, there was the honor of the Turners! So I sneaked out, with my heart in my boots,— your boots, I mean,—and Hop called for a line play, and then another one, and I thought maybe I was going to get off without making a fool of myself. But no such luck. 'Take all the time you want, Nid,' said Hop. 'We'll hold 'em for you. Drop it over, for the love of mud! We've got to have this game!' 'Drop it?' said I. 'Not on your life, Hop! Make it a place-kick or I'll never have a chance!' 'What do you mean?' he asked. 'I mean I can't drop-kick to-day.' I guess something in my voice or the way I said it put him on, for he looked at me pretty sharp. Still, maybe he didn't guess the truth, either, for he let me have my way and let me kick.

"After that"—Laurie half closed his eyes and shook his head slowly—"after that I don't really know what did happen. I have a sort of a hazy recollection of Hop shouting some signals that didn't mean a thing in my young life, and kneeling on the ground a couple of yards ahead of me. I didn't dare look at the goal, though I knew it was ahead of me and about twenty yards away. Then there was a brown streak, and things began to move, and I moved with them. I suppose I swung my foot,-probably my right one, though it may have been my left,—and then I closed my eyes tight and waited for some one to kill me. Next thing I knew, I was being killed—or I thought I thought I was, for a second. It turned out, though, that the fellows weren't really killing me; they were just beating me black and blue to show they were pleased.

"Of course, it was all the biggest piece of luck that ever happened, Ned. Hop aimed the ball just right, and somehow or other I managed to kick it. Maybe any one would have done just as well, because I guess it was an easy goal. Anyway, the honor of the Turners was safe!"

"You're a regular brick," said Ned, a bit huskily. "What—what happened afterward? I didn't stay."

"Afterward Hop looked at me kind of queer and said, 'I guess that'll do for you, Turner,' and I beat it away from there as fast as I knew how, and Mulford sent in some other poor unfortunate. There were only half a dozen plays after that, and we kicked whenever we got the ball."

"Do you think any one but Hop found out?" asked Ned, anxiously.

"Not a one. And I'm not sure, mind you, that Hop did. You see, he didn't *say* anything. Only, he did call me 'Nid' at first, and then 'Turner' the next time. I haven't seen him since. I guess I never will know, unless I ask him. One thing's sure, though, Ned, and that is that Hop won't talk."

"You don't think I'd ought to fess up?" asked Ned.

"I do not," replied Laurie stoutly. "What's the good? It wasn't your fault if you went to sleep out in the country. If any one's to blame, it's me. I oughtn't to have hoaxed them. No, sir; if Mulford or any one says anything, just you tell them you fell asleep and couldn't help getting there late. But I don't believe any one will ask questions now. They're all too pleased and excited. But, gee, Neddie! I certainly am glad I made that goal instead of missing it. I'd be a pretty mean feeling pup to-night if I hadn't!"

"It was wonderful," mused Ned. "You putting it over, I mean. With all that crowd looking on, and Farview shouting—"

"Shouting? I didn't hear them. I didn't know whether there was any one around just then! I had troubles of my own, partner! Know something? Well, I think there's the chap who kicked that goal." Laurie raised his right foot and displayed one of Ned's scuffed football shoes. "I guess I just sort of left things to him and he did the business. Good old Mister Shoe!"

Ned jumped to his feet and pulled Laurie from the bed. "For the love of lemons," he cried, "get those togs off before any one comes in!"

"Gee, that's so!" Laurie worked feverishly, while Ned stumbled over a chair and turned the key in the lock.

"A fine pair of idiots we are!" exclaimed Ned, as he ripped Laurie's shirt off for him. "Suppose Hop or Kewpie had come in while we were sitting here!"

Hillman's spent the rest of the evening in celebration. In the dining-hall the appearance of any member of the squad was the signal for hand-clapping and cheers, and when Ned entered, followed by Laurie, the applause was deafening. Ned showed himself to be a very modest and retiring hero, for he fairly scuttled to his seat, and kept his head bent over his plate long after the applause had died away. Then, stealing an unhappy glance at Laurie, he found that youth grinning broadly, and was the recipient of a most meaningful wink. After supper, in the corridor, the twins ran squarely into Hop Kendrick. Ned tried to pull aside, but Laurie stood his ground. Hop was plainly a very happy youth to-night, although even when happiest he never entirely lost his look of earnest gravity.

"Well, we did it, Nid!" he said joyfully, clapping that youth on the shoulder. "That was a corking kick of yours, son!"

Ned stammered something utterly unintelligible, but Laurie came to the rescue: "Ned says it was the way you pointed the ball that won that goal, Hop," he said casually. "He's mighty modest about it."

Hop shot a quick glance at the speaker, and Ned declared afterward that there was a smile behind it. But all he said was: "Oh, well, pointing isn't everything, Nod. *Some one's* got to kick it!"

When he had gone on, Ned and Laurie viewed each other questioningly. "Think he knows?" asked Ned. Laurie shook his head frowningly. "You've got me, partner!" he answered.

And, because neither asked Hop Kendrick outright, neither ever did know!

There were songs and speeches and a general jollification after supper, ending in a parade of cheering, singing youths who marched through the town from end to end, and at last drew up outside Doctor Hillman's porch and shouted until that gentleman appeared and responded. The Doctor's words were few, but they hit the spot, and when there had been another long cheer for him, and another long cheer for the team, and a final mighty cheer for the school, the happy boys called it a day and sought the dormitories.

Ned was just dropping off to sleep that night when Laurie's voice reached him through the darkness.

"Ned!" called Laurie.

"Huh?"

"Are you awake?"

"Uh-huh."

"Listen. It's a fortunate thing to be a twin."

There was a long moment of silence. Then Ned's voice came sleepily:

"'Cause if one twin can't the other twin kin!"

CHAPTER XXII
THE BOYS MAKE A PRESENT

The week or so succeeding the Farview game seemed like an anticlimax. The bottom had sort of dropped out of things and there was no immediate excitement to look forward to. The weather became as miserable as weather possibly could, the slight snowfall that followed the rain of Thanksgiving Day lasting only long enough to be seen by the early risers. Perhaps it was well that lack of events and inclement weather ruled, for Ned and a good many other boys in school were no worse for an opportunity to apply themselves undisturbedly to their studies. Basketball candidates were called the first Monday in December, and the twins held a serious conference on the question of reporting. Ned, who felt rather flat since there was no more football, was half inclined to go in for the game, and would have had Laurie insisted. But Laurie voted that for the present the Turners had done sufficient in the athletic line, that the honor of the family demanded no further sacrifices on the altar of duty. So Ned abandoned the idea and talked of trying for the crew in the spring.

When December was a week old, the fellows set their gaze on the Christmas recess, which this year began on Wednesday, three days before Christmas, and lasted until the 2d of January. Eleven days are not sufficient to make a trip across the continent and back advisable, although the twins figured that, with the best of fortune, they would be able to reach Santa Lucia in time for dinner Christmas night. On the other hand, the missing of one connection would delay their arrival until the following afternoon, and, as Laurie pointed out, they were fairly certain to be held up somewhere on the way, and a sleeping-car wasn't exactly an ideal place in which to spend the holiday! Besides, there was a noticeable lack of encouragement from home. It had been accepted beforehand that the boys were to remain at the school during the recess, and nothing in Mr. Turner's fortnightly letters hinted that he had changed his mind.

"I'd just as lief stay here, anyway," declared Ned. "We can have a lot more fun. Maybe there'll be a bunch of snow, and I'm dying to try skiing."

"You bet! And skating, too! And then there's that other scheme. Mustn't forget that, Neddie."

"You mean—"

"Yes. Didn't you say we'd do it during vacation?"

"Sure! It—it'll take quite a lot of money, though, Laurie. And we'll have presents to buy for Dad and Aunt Emmie and the cousins—"

"The cousins get Christmas cards, and that's all they do get," interrupted Laurie, decisively. "That's all they ever give us, and I'd rather spend my money on something that'll really—really benefit some one. I guess Dad'll send us some more money, too, for Christmas. We can do it, all right. I've got nearly seven dollars right now. I haven't spent hardly any money this month."

"All right. Some day soon we'll go downtown and find out how much it's going to cost and what we'll need and everything. I say, we can get Bob to help us, too!"

"Rather! And three or four other fellows, I guess. Every one likes the Widow, and George says there will be five or six fellows here during recess. He was here last year, and he says he had a dandy time."

"Let's get George this afternoon and get the thing started. We can find out the—the area and ask the man how much we'll need."

"Sure! And we can buy it and store it at Bob's. Then all we'll have to do will be carry it over the fence. I'll go down and see if I can find him. Look here, Neddie. Why don't we do it before Christmas and make it a sort of Christmas present? Say we worked hard all day Thursday and Friday—"

"Great! Only if it snowed—"

Laurie's face fell. "Gee, that's so! I suppose we couldn't do it if it snowed. Or rained. Or if it was frightfully cold."

"They say it doesn't get real cold here until after New Year's," said Ned, reassuringly. "But of course it might snow or rain. Well, we'll do it in time for Christmas if we can. If we can't, we'll do it for New Year's. I'll bet she'll be tickled to death. I say, though! We never found out about the color!"

"I did," answered Laurie modestly. "I asked Polly. She said white."

"White! Geewhillikins, Laurie, that makes it harder, doesn't it? We'd have to put on two coats!"

"Think so?" Laurie frowned. "I guess we would. That would take twice as long, eh? Look here; maybe—maybe I can get Polly to change her mind!"

"That's likely, you chump!" Ned scowled thoughtfully. Finally, "I tell you what," he said. "Suppose we went around there sometime, and talked with Mrs. Deane, and told her how nice we think blue looks and how sort of—of distinctive! Gee, it wouldn't be any trick at all to make it blue; but white—" He shook his head despondently.

"Cheer up!" said Laurie. "I've got the dope, partner! Listen. We'll tell them that it ought to be blue because blue's the school color and all that. Mrs.

Deane thinks a heap of Hillman's, and she'll fall for it as sure as shooting. So'll Polly! Come on! Let's find George and get the thing started!"

"Better get Bob to go with us, too. He said something about wanting to pay his share of it, so we'd better let him in right from the start. After all, we don't want to hog it, Laurie!"

A fortnight later the exodus came. Of the four-score lads who lived at Hillman's, all but eight took their departure that Wednesday morning, and Ned and Laurie and George watched the last group drive off for the station with feelings of genuine satisfaction. Life at school during the eleven days of recess promised to be busy and enjoyable, and they were eager to see the decks cleared, so to speak, and to start the new way of living. Ned and Laurie had had plenty of invitations for Christmas week. Both Kewpie and Lee Murdock had earnestly desired their society at their respective homes, and there had been others less insistent but possibly quite as cordial invitations. But neither one had weakened. George half promised one of the boys to visit him for a few days after Christmas, but later he canceled his acceptance.

Besides George and the twins, there remained at school five other fellows who, because they lived at a distance and railway fares were high, or for other reasons, found it expedient to accept Doctor Hillman's hospitality. None of the five, two juniors, one lower middler, and two upper middlers, were known to the twins more than casually when recess began; but eating together three times a day and being thrown in one another's society at other times soon made the acquaintance much closer, and all proved to be decent, likable chaps.

Meals were served at a corner table in West Hall, and during recess there were seldom fewer than three of the faculty present. That may sound depressing, but in vacation-time an instructor becomes quite a human, jovial person, and the scant dozen around the table enjoyed themselves hugely. In the evening Doctor Hillman held open house, and Miss Tabitha showed a genius for providing methods of entertainment. Sometimes they popped corn in the fireplace in the cozy living-room, sometimes they roasted apples. Once it was chestnuts that jumped on the hearth. Then, too, Miss Tabitha was a past mistress in the art of making fudge, and on two occasions Mr. Barrett, the mathematics instructor, displayed such a sweet tooth that the boys lost the last of their awe and "ragged" him without mercy. Several times the Doctor read aloud, choosing, to the boys' surprise, a corking detective novel that had them squirming on the edges of their chairs. Toward the last of the vacation, Laurie confided to Ned and George that he wished recess was just beginning.

To Ned's and Laurie's great disappointment, neither snow nor ice appeared and the weather remained merely briskly cold, with sometimes a day like

Indian summer. But I am getting ahead of my story, which really comes to an end on Christmas Day.

More than a week before the closing of school, the four conspirators had finished their preparations for the task that was to provide the Widow Deane with a novel Christmas present. In Bob's cellar were many cans containing blue paint, white paint, linseed oil, and turpentine. There were brushes there, too, and a scraper, and a roll of cotton rags provided by Polly. For, in the end, it had become necessary to acquaint Polly with the project. Against Bob's back fence reposed all the ladders, of varying lengths, that the neighborhood afforded. Wednesday evening Ned and Laurie and George herded the other boys into George's room, and explained the scheme and asked for volunteers. They got five most enthusiastic ones.

Nine o'clock the next morning was set as the time for the beginning of the work, and at that hour nine rather disreputably-attired youths appeared in Mrs. Deane's yard, arriving by way of the back fence, and began their assault. The first the Widow knew of what was happening was when, being then occupied with the task of tidying up the sleeping-room on the second floor, she was startled to see the head and shoulders of a boy appear outside her window. Her exclamation of alarm gave place to murmurs of bewilderment as the supposed burglar contented himself with lifting the two shutters from their hinges and passing them down the ladder to some unseen accomplice. Mrs. Deane looked forth. In the garden was what at first glimpse looked like a convention of tramps. They were armed with ladders and brushes and pots of paint, and they were already very busy. Across two trestles set on the grass plot, the stolen shutters were laid as fast as they were taken down. One boy, flourishing a broad-bladed implement, scraped the rough surfaces. A second plied a big round brush, dusting diligently. Numbers three and four, as soon as the first two operatives retired, attacked with brushes dripping with white paint. In almost no time at all the first shutter was off the trestles and leaning, fresh and spotless, against the fence. Every instant another shutter appeared. Mrs. Deane gazed in fascinated amazement. One after another, she recognized the miscreants: the two Turner boys, George Watson, Mr. Starling's son, Hal Goring, the Stanton boy, and the rest; but, although recognition brought reassurance, bewilderment remained, and she hurried downstairs as fast as ever she could go.

Polly was on the back porch, a very disturbed and somewhat indignant Towser in her arms, evidently a party to the undertaking, and to her Mrs. Deane breathlessly appealed.

"Polly! What are they doing?" she gasped.

"You'll have to ask the boys, Mama." Polly's eyes were dancing. "Nid, here's Mama, and she wants to know what you're doing!"

Nid hurried up, a dripping brush in one hand and a smear of white paint across one cheek, followed by Laurie. The others paused at their various tasks to watch smilingly.

"Painting the house, Mrs. Deane!"

"Painting the house! My house? Why—why—what—who—"

"Yes'm. There's the blue paint. It's as near like the old as we could find. You don't think it's too dark, do you?"

"But I don't understand, Nid Turner!" said Mrs. Deane helplessly. "Who told you to? Who's going to pay for it?"

"It's all paid for, ma'am. It—it's a sort of Christmas present from us—from the school. You—you don't mind, do you?"

"Well, I never did!" Mrs. Deane looked from Ned to Laurie, her mouth quivering. "I—I don't know what to say. I guess I'll—I'll go see if any one's—in the shop, Polly. Did you think you—heard the bell?" Mrs. Deane's eyes were frankly wet as she turned hurriedly away and disappeared inside. Ned viewed Polly anxiously.

"Do you think she—doesn't like it?" he half whispered.

Polly shook her head and laughed softly, although her own eyes were not quite dry. "Of course she likes it, you stupid boy! She just didn't know what to say. She'll be back pretty soon, after she's had a little cry."

"Oh!" said Ned and Laurie in chorus, their faces brightening; and Laurie added apologetically: "Gee, we didn't want to make her cry, Polly!"

"That sort of a cry doesn't hurt," said Polly.

Afterward Mrs. Deane said a great deal, and said it very sweetly, and the boys got more or less embarrassed, and were heartily glad when she drew Ned to her and kissed him, much to that youth's distress, and the incident ended in laughter. By noon the shutters were done, and nine industrious amateur painters were swarming over the back of the little house. I'm not going to tell you that the job was done as perfectly as Sprague and Currie, Painters and Paper-hangers, would have done it, but you're to believe that it was done much quicker and at a far greater saving of money! And when it was finished no one except a professional would ever have known the difference. Perhaps there was more blue and white paint scattered around the landscape than was absolutely necessary, and it always remained a mystery how Antoinette managed to get her right ear looking like a bit of Italian sky, for every one professed ignorance and Antoinette was apparently well protected from spatters. (It took Polly more than a week to restore the rabbit to her original appearance.)

When the early winter twilight fell and it became necessary to knock off work for the day, the blue painting was more than half done and, unless weather prevented, it was certain that the entire task would be finished by to-morrow evening. Mrs. Deane served five-o'clock tea,—only it happened to be four-o'clock tea instead,—and nine very, very hungry lads did full justice to the repast, and the little room behind the store held a merry party. Perhaps the prevailing odor of paint detracted somewhat from Mrs. Deane's and Polly's enjoyment of the refreshments, but you may be certain they made no mention of the fact.

That night the boys viewed the cloudy sky apprehensively. Laurie, who knew little about it, declared dubiously that it smelt like snow. But when morning came, although the cloudiness persisted most of the day, the weather remained kindly, with just enough frost in the air to chill feet and nip idle fingers and to give an added zest to labor. Very little time was wasted on luncheon, and at two o'clock the last slap of blue paint had been applied and the more difficult work of doing the white trim began. Fortunately, there were only eleven windows and two doors, and although "drawing" the sashes was slow and finicking work, with nine willing hands hard at it the end came shortly after dusk, when, watched by eight impatient companions, young Haskell, one of the junior class boys, with trembling fingers drew his brush along the last few inches of a front window, and then, because he was quite keyed up and because it was much too dark to see well, celebrated the culmination of his efforts by putting a foot squarely into a can of white paint!

When first-aid methods had been applied, he was allowed, on promise to put only one foot to the floor, to accompany the rest inside and announce to a delighted and slightly tremulous Mrs. Deane that the work was completed. There was a real celebration then, with more piping-hot tea and lots of perfectly scrumptious cream-puffs,—besides less enticing bread-and-butter sandwiches,—and Mrs. Deane tried hard to thank the boys and couldn't quite do it, and Polly failed almost as dismally, and Laurie made a wonderful speech that no one understood very well, except for the general meaning, and nine flushed and very happy youths cheered long and loudly for Mrs. Deane, and finally departed merrily into the winter twilight, calling back many a "Merry Christmas" as they went.

CHAPTER XXIII
THE SECRET PASSAGE

Christmas Day dawned clear and mild, a green Christmas if ever there was one. And yet, in spite of the absence of such traditional accompaniments as snow and ice, the spirit of the season was there in abundance. Ned and Laurie, wakening early to the sound of church bells, felt Christmasy right from the first conscious moment. When they hastened down the hall for their baths, they could hear George and Hal Goring on the floor below uniting in what they fondly believed was song. Later, at breakfast, beside a perfectly wonderful repast in which chicken and little crisp sausages and hot, crisp waffles played leading rôles, the Doctor and Miss Tabitha had placed at each plate a Christmas card tied by a tiny blue ribbon to a diminutive painter's brush! Later on there was to be a tree in the Doctor's living-room. In fact, the tree was already there, and the boys had spent much of the preceding evening trimming it and placing around its base inexpensive gifts of a joking nature for one another and the Doctor and Miss Tabitha and the two instructors who were there.

Laurie and Ned had exchanged presents with each other and had received several from home, not the least welcome of which was a check from their father. And they had bought small gifts for George and Bob. Also, though you needn't tell it around school, Laurie had purchased a most odoriferous and ornate bottle of perfume for Polly! So when, shortly after breakfast, Ned suggested that Laurie take Bob's present over to him, Laurie evinced entire willingness to perform the errand. That he carried not one gift but two in his pockets was, however, beyond Ned's knowledge. A cheerful whistling from the back of the house drew Laurie past the front entrance, and he found Bob, attired in any but festal garments, swinging open the bulkhead doors. A pair of old gray trousers and a disreputable brown sweater formed most of his costume. At sight of Laurie he gave a joyful whoop.

"Merry Christmas!" he called. "I was going over to see you in a minute. Thomas is in bed with a cold or something, and I'm furnace-man and general factotle—"

"Factotum, you mean," laughed Laurie.

"All right! As you fellows say, what do I care? I don't own it. Now you're here, you can just give me a hand with this load of junk. Dad says it doesn't look shipshape for Christmas." Bob indicated more than a dozen paint-cans, empty, partly empty, or unopened, and a mess of brushes, paddles, and rags that they had set there last evening. "I suppose a lot of these might as well be thrown away, but we'll dump the whole caboodle down in the cellar for now."

"All right," agreed Laurie. "First, though, here's something that Ned and I thought you might like. It isn't anything much, you know, Bob; just a—a trinket."

"For me?" Bob took the little packet, and removed the paper and then the lid, disclosing a pair of silver cuff-links lying in a nest of cotton-wool. As Laurie said, they weren't much, but they were neat and the jeweler had made a very good job of the three plain block letters, R. D. S., that he had engraved on them. "Gee, they're corking!" exclaimed Bob, with unmistakable sincerity. "I needed them, too, Nod. I lost one of a pair just the other day, and—"

"I know you did. That's why we got those."

"Well, I'm awfully much obliged. They're great. I've got a couple of little things upstairs for you chaps. They aren't nearly so nice as these, but I'll get 'em—"

"Wait till we finish this job," said Laurie. "Grab a handful and come on. Is Thomas very sick?"

"I guess not," replied Bob, as he followed the other down the steps. "He ate some breakfast, but aunt thought he'd better stay in bed. I had a great time with the furnace this morning. Got up at half-past six and shoveled coal to beat the band!"

"Where do you want to put these?" asked Laurie.

"Anywhere, I guess. Hold on; let's dump 'em on the shelves in the closet there. Then they'll be out of the way. Some day we'll clean the cans all out, and maybe we'll get enough to paint that arbor we're going to build. Here you are."

Bob led the way to a small room built against the rear wall of the big cellar. Designed for a preserve closet, its shelves had probably long been empty of aught save dust, and the door, wide open, hung from one hinge. It was some six feet broad and perhaps five feet deep, built of matched boards. Before Bob entered the cobwebby doorway with his load of cans, its only contents were an accumulation of empty preserve-jars in a wooden box set on the cement floor beneath a lower shelf at the back. There were eight shelves across the rear wall, divided in the center by a vertical board into two tiers. Bob placed his load on a lower shelf and Laurie put his on the shelf above. As he drew away he noticed that the shelf appeared to have worked out from the boards at the back, and he gave it a blow on the edge with the flat of one hand. It slipped back into place, but, to his surprise, it came forward again an inch or two, and all the other shelves in that tier came with it!

"Hey!" said Laurie, startled.

Bob, at the doorway, turned. "What's the matter?" he asked.

"Nothing, only—" Laurie took hold of the shelf above the loosened one and pulled. It yielded a little, and so did the other shelves and the rear wall of the cubicle, but it was only a matter of less than an inch. Bob, at his side, looked on interestedly.

"That's funny," he said. "Push on it."

Laurie pushed, and the tier went back a couple of inches. "Looks like this side was separate from the rest," said Laurie. "What's the idea of having it come out like that?"

"Search me!" answered Bob. "Pull it toward you again and let me have a look." A second later he exclaimed: "The whole side is loose, Nod, but it can't come out because the ends of the shelves strike this partition board! Try it again!" Laurie obeyed, moving the tier back and forth three or four times as far as it would go. Bob shook his head in puzzlement, his gaze roving around the dim interior. Then, "Look here," he said. "The shelves on the side aren't on a level with the back ones, Nod."

"What of it?"

"Nothing, maybe; only, if the back swung out the side shelves wouldn't stop it! See what I mean?"

"Not exactly. Anyhow, it doesn't swing out, so what's the—"

"Hold on!" Bob sprang forward and seized the edge of a shelf in the right-hand tier close to the partition board, and pulled. It readily yielded an inch, but no more.

"Wait!" Laurie bent and pulled aside the box of jars. "Now!"

Then, as Bob tugged, to their amazement the right-hand tier swung toward them, its lower edge scraping on the cement floor, and the left-hand tier swung with it, the whole back wall of the closet, shelves and all, opening toward them like a pair of double doors!

"Gee!" whispered Laurie. "What do you suppose—"

"Pull them wide open and let's find out," said Bob recklessly.

When the two sides were open as far as they would go, there was an aperture between them some three feet wide. Beyond it was darkness, though, as they gazed, the stones of the cellar wall took shape dimly. Then Laurie seized Bob's arm.

"Look!" he whispered excitedly. Behind, where the left-hand tier of shelves had stood, was a blacker patch about three feet high by two feet wide, which, as they stared in fascination, evolved itself into an opening in the wall.

"Know what I think?" asked Bob, in low tones. "I think we've found the miser's hiding-place, Nod!"

"Honest? Maybe it's just a—a drain or something. Got a match?"

"There are some over by the furnace. Hold your horses!" Bob hurried out, and was back in a moment and was standing at the opening between the doors with a lighted match held toward the opening in the wall. As the little light grew they saw that the stones of the wall had been removed from a space of a foot above the floor and three feet high and some two feet wide. Around the opening so made cement had been applied in the form of a smooth casing.

The match flickered and went out, and in the succeeding gloom the two boys stared at each other with wide eyes.

"Would you dare go in there?" asked Laurie.

"Sure! Why not? It can't be anything but a sort of cave underground. Wait till I get a candle."

"A lantern would be better," suggested Laurie, viewing the hole dubiously.

"That's so, and there's one here somewhere. I noticed it the other day." Bob's voice came from the cellar beyond, and Laurie heard him walking around out there. Then, "I've got it!" Bob called. "There's oil in it, too! Now we'll have a look!"

Laurie heard the chimney of the lantern squeak as it was forced up and then drop into place again. Then a wan light came toward the closet, and Bob appeared, triumphant and excited. "Wait till I turn it up a bit. There we are! Come on!"

They passed through between the doors, Bob leading, and stooped before the hole in the wall. Bob held the lantern inside, and Laurie peered over his shoulder. "Gee, it's high," whispered the latter.

"Yes, and it isn't a cave at all; it's a tunnel!" said Bob, in awed tones. "What do you say?"

"I'll go, if you will," replied Laurie, stoutly; and without much enthusiasm Bob ducked his head and crawled through. Past the two-foot wall was a passage, more than head-high and about a yard in width, stone walled and arched, that led straight ahead farther than the light of the lantern penetrated.

The walls were dry, but the earthen floor was damp to the touch. There was a musty odor, though the air in there seemed fresh.

"Where do you suppose it goes to?" asked Bob, in a hushed voice.

"I can't imagine. But it runs straight back from the cellar, and so it must pass under the garden. Let's—let's go on, Bob."

"Sure! Only I thought we were going to find old Coventry's treasure!"

"How do you know we aren't?" asked Laurie.

"That's so! Maybe he buried it under the garden." Their footfalls sounded clearly on the hard-packed earth floor as they went ahead. Suddenly Bob, in the lead, uttered an exclamation, and Laurie jumped a foot and then hurried forward to where the other was standing. Beside him, its point buried in the floor of the tunnel, was the lost crowbar!

"What do you know?" gasped Bob. "We're under the farther end of the arbor. That bar came through between those stones up here." He touch the crevice in the arched roof with a finger. "See the dirt it brought down with it? Well, that explains that mystery!"

"Yes, but—where does this thing go to, Bob?"

"Let's find out. It can't go much farther, because the arbor was only about forty feet from the back fence."

But they went that forty feet and perhaps forty more before the wavering light of the lantern showed them a stout wooden door across their path. Formed of two-inch planking and strengthened with three broad cleats, it was hinged to a frame of concrete. It wasn't a big door, but it looked very formidable to the two boys who stood there and viewed it dubiously in the yellow glare of the lantern; for a big square iron lock held it firmly in place.

"Guess we don't go any farther," said Bob, dryly.

"Maybe the key's here somewhere," Laurie suggested; and, although Bob scoffed at the suggestion, they searched thoroughly but without success.

"We could bust it," Bob said; "only maybe we haven't any right to."

"I don't see why not, Bob. We discovered it. Let's!"

"We-ell, but one of us'll have to go for a hammer or something."

"Sure; I'll go."

"And leave me here in the dark? I guess not!"

"We'll both go, then. Hold on! What's the matter with the crowbar?"

"Of course! I never thought of that! I'll fetch it!" The light receded down the tunnel until it was small and dim, and Laurie, left alone in front of the mysterious portal, felt none too happy. Of course there was nothing to be afraid of, but he was awfully glad when the light drew nearer again and Bob returned. "You hold this," directed Bob, "and I'll give it a couple of whacks."

Laurie took the lantern, and Bob brought the bar down smartly on the lock. Probably it was old and rusty, for it broke into pieces under the blow, and in another instant they had thrust the heavy bolt back. Then Bob took a long breath and pulled the door toward them. The hinges squeaked loudly, startlingly, in the silence. Before them lay darkness, and Laurie, leaning past the doorway, raised the lantern high.

CHAPTER XXIV
A MERRY CHRISTMAS

"Guess Laurie got lost," grumbled Ned, kicking one foot against the step and looking across the yard.

George laughed. "Guess you could find him if you went as far as the Widow's, Nid."

"Well, he ought to be back. It's nearly time for the tree, isn't it?" Characteristically, Ned saved himself the trouble of determining the matter for himself, and it was George who looked at his watch.

"There's 'most an hour yet. Let's go and have a look for him. He and Bob are probably at Polly's."

But they didn't get as far as Polly's just then, for when they reached the corner they descried Laurie tearing along the side yard of the Coventry place. At sight of them he moderated his speed slightly and began to shout, waving both hands in a quite demented manner.

"What's he saying?" asked George. "What's wrong?"

"Wants us to hurry," grumbled Ned. "We are hurrying, you idiot!" he continued, raising his voice. But he hurried faster, George at his heels, and met Laurie at the front gate.

"What's your trouble?" he demanded. "House on fire? Bob got the croup? What is it? Can't you talk?"

"Can't tell you," panted Laurie. "You've got to see—for yourself! Come on!"

He seized Ned by one arm, and pulled him away and around the house and down the bulkhead steps, George loping after them. In the cellar stood Bob, disreputable in his old clothes and adorned with dust and cobwebs, a lighted lantern in one hand.

"Has he told you?" he cried, as the others piled down the stairs.

"Told me? He hasn't told anything," gasped Ned, shaking himself free at last. "What is it?"

Bob laughed loudly and gleefully. "Then come on!" he shouted. He dashed into the preserve closet, Ned, George, and Laurie at his heels, passed from sight for an instant, and was seen again crawling through a hole in the wall. Ned and George showered questions as they pattered along the tunnel, but all they received in reply was insane laughter and a meaningless, breathless jumble of words. And then they were at the farther portal, and Bob led the way through, and they followed.

They found themselves in a small cellar-like compartment scarcely four paces square. It was windowless, although, close to the raftered ceiling in the rear wall, two oblongs of brick set in the stone showed where at some time small windows had been. The floor was paved with flat stones. In one corner, the only objects there, were a small iron chest, its lid swung open and back, and a crowbar. The newcomers stared in amazement, the truth slowly dawning on them. It was Laurie who spoke first.

"Go and look!" he said excitedly.

Ned and George obeyed. Within the chest lay four fat, heavy brownish envelopes, bound and tied with pink tape.

"Take one out and open it," said Bob over Ned's shoulder.

Ned picked up one. Across one end was written in scrawly characters the inscription "Gov't."

"'Government,'" explained Laurie, softly. "It's full of United States bonds. Nearly a dozen of them. Have a look."

"Geewhillikins!" breathed Ned, in awe, as he drew the folded contents into the light. "Old Coventry's, do you mean?"

"Of course! Whose else? And there are three more lots. We haven't figured them up yet, but there must be fifty thousand dollars' worth!"

"Maybe they're no good," offered George.

"How do you mean, no good?" asked Ned indignantly. "United States bonds are always good!"

"Well, the others—"

"They're railroad bonds, all of them, three different lots," said Bob. "I guess they're all right, too, don't you, Ned?"

"Right as rain! Why, the old codger—What's that?" he asked suddenly, looking ceiling-ward. Laurie laughed.

"That's what we wondered," he answered. "We jumped when we heard it first. Don't you know where you are?"

Ned looked around him and shook his head.

"Under the Widow Deane's house!"

"Wha-at! But Polly said there wasn't any cellar!"

"She doesn't know any better. Look above you. See where the stairway went? The old chap must have torn it away and boarded the hole up; and bricked up the windows, too. It must have cost him a pretty penny to do all this!"

"What—what are you going to do with it?" asked George, pointing to the chest.

"Why, hand it over to the lawyers, whoever they are, I suppose," answered Bob. "But first of all we're going to take those bonds and dump them into the Widow's lap. I always said I'd hand it all over to her, when I found it. I never thought I would find it, but I have—or Laurie has, because if he hadn't noticed that the shelves were loose we never would—"

"Besides," interrupted George, "she comes in for a share of the money. Come on, fellows! Let's do it now! Gee, it will be some Christmas present!"

"Won't it? Let's each one take a package," said Laurie. "We'll leave everything just as it is for the lawyer folks. Come on!"

"Say, fellows, there's an awfully funny smell down here," observed George. "Sort of—sort of sweet, like—like violets or something. Notice it?"

"Yes, I noticed it before I got in here, though," said Ned. "Wonder what it is."

"Oh, places like this get to smelling funny after they've been shut up for a while," said Bob. "And I guess this place hasn't been opened for two years, eh?"

"Of course not; not since old Coventry died. Just the same, it's a mighty funny odor." And George sniffed again perplexedly. Laurie, who had withdrawn to the door, unconsciously placed a hand in one jacket pocket, where, within a crushed cardboard box, some fragments of glass were all that remained of Polly's present! In prying open the lid of the chest he had brought the end of the crowbar against that pocket, and now the purchase was only a memory, albeit a fragrant one.

Some three minutes later four flushed-faced and very joyous youths burst into the Widow Deane's shop. To the jangling of the little bell in the back room Polly appeared, a very pretty, bright-eyed Polly this morning in a new Christmas dress.

"Merry Christmas!" she cried. "Merry Christmas, Nid! Merry Christmas, Bob! Merry Christmas, George! Merry Christmas, Nod!"

Perhaps Laurie should have felt hurt that his own greeting had come last; but he wasn't, for a glance went with it that hadn't accompanied the others. But, although the boys answered the greetings in chorus, it was apparent to Polly that they were there for another purpose than to wish her a Merry Christmas.

"Where's your mother!" demanded Bob.

"In there." Polly pointed to the back room, and without ceremony the four filed past and into the little living-room. Mrs. Deane was seated in a rocker, her spectacles pushed down on her nose, a paper across her knees, and her eyes fixed in smiling inquiry on the doorway.

Bob led the way. On the outspread paper he laid a brown envelop. "Wish you a Merry Christmas, ma'am," he said.

Laurie followed, deposited his envelop beside Bob's, repeated the greeting, and drew aside to make way for Nod and George. The Widow looked inquiringly from the stout envelops to the boys, smiling tolerantly the while. Boys were always up to pranks, and she liked them, boys and pranks both!

"What are these?" she asked, finally, when the fourth envelop lay in her lap.

Polly, looking over her shoulder, gasped as she read the writing on one of the packets, and her eyes, as round as round, looked across at Laurie.

"*Nod! They aren't—You haven't—*"

"Yes, they are!" cried Laurie. "Look and see for yourself! Open them, Mrs. Deane!"

Ten minutes later, when the first excitement had somewhat subsided, Polly clapped her hands.

"Why," she cried, "now we know what those sounds were we used to hear, Mama! They were Uncle Peter down there in the cellar! They were his footsteps! And only a little while ago I thought I heard sounds sort of like them! And that must have been you boys!"

"Of course," agreed Bob. "And we could hear you folks up here quite plainly. There goes my last hope of catching a ghost!"

"How many are there to share in the money, Mrs. Deane?" asked George.

"Dear me, I'm not quite sure." She looked inquiringly over her spectacles at Polly. "Weren't there seven, dear?"

"Eight, Mama."

"Well, even then it isn't so bad" said George. "One eighth of sixty-two-thousand—"

"Seven thousand seven hundred and fifty," announced Laurie, promptly. "And the bonds may be worth more than we figured, ma'am!"

"Well, I'm sure," answered Mrs. Deane, "seven thousand dollars is seven times more money than I ever expected to see! I shan't know what to do with it." She looked quite alarmed and helpless for a moment, but Polly patted her shoulder reassuringly.

"You must invest it, dearest, and then you won't have to keep this place any longer, because when I go to work—"

But, instead of vanishing, the Widow Deane's alarm increased. "Oh, I couldn't give up the store, Polly!" she gasped. "Why—why, what would I do with myself all day?"

"Yes'm that's so!" declared Ned, heartily. "Gee, you couldn't do that! Why, we wouldn't have any place to buy cream-puffs!"

"I guess I would keep on with the store," Mrs. Deane concluded, when the laughter had subsided. "I'm afraid I'd never be very happy if I didn't have you boys around. Well, it's certainly very wonderful, isn't it, Polly?"

"It's—it's heavenly!" declared Polly. "This is just the most beautiful Christmas there ever was or ever will be! And I don't see how we can ever thank you all for finding—"

"Gosh!" exclaimed Laurie. "The Doctor's tree, fellows! We'll have to beat it! We'll leave the bonds here until to-morrow—eh?"

"But I want to see the tunnel and—and everything!" cried Polly.

"That's so! We'll come over after dinner. Come on, fellows! Neddie, come away from those tarts!"

"I was only looking," sighed Ned.

Mrs. Deane and Polly went with them to the door. Down the street the deep-toned bell in the Congregational church was ringing, and, farther away, other bells were joining in a chorus of glad triumph. Mrs. Deane, listening, held a very happy look in her face. On the sidewalk, Ned and Laurie dropped behind their companions, paused, and faced the doorway. There was a quick exchange of glances between them, and then, bowing, Ned began and Laurie finished:

> "A Merry Christmas and well-filled bins,"
> "Is the hearty wish of the Turner Twins!"

———————